D0109665

MARGHERITA DOLCE VITA

Stefano Benni

MARGHERITA DOLCE VITA

Translated from the Italian
by Antony Shugaar

Europa
editions

Europa Editions
116 East 16th Street
New York, N.Y. 10003
www.europaeditions.com
info@europaeditions.com

Copyright © 2005 by Giangiacomo Feltrinelli Editore, Milano
First Publication 2006 by Europa Editions

Translation by Antony Shugaar
Original title: *Margherita Dolcevita*
Translation copyright © 2006 by Europa Editions

Library of Congress Cataloging in Publication Data is available
ISBN 1-933372-20-6

Benni, Stefano
Margherita Dolce Vita

Book design by Emanuele Ragnisco
www.mekkanografici.com

Printed in Italy
Arti Grafiche La Moderna – Rome

CONTENTS

*Sometimes, in a shaft of sunlight pouring
through a window, we see life in the air.
And we call it dust.*

*The world is divided into:
Those who eat chocolate without bread;
Those who can't eat chocolate unless it's
with bread;
Those who have no chocolate
Those who have no bread.*

(From the famous sayings of
Grandpa Socrates)

1. The Night the Stars Vanished

I climbed into bed, and the stars had vanished. I carefully cleaned the window pane, but it did no good. The stars were gone. Sirius had disappeared. So had Venus and Carmilla and Althazor. And Mab and Zelda and Bakbuk and Dandelion, along with the constellation of the Turkey and Lennon's Cross.

You needn't tell me that some of these stars don't exist. Those are my own names for them. In fact, I defend the right of anyone—especially an imaginative young girl like me—to call things not only by the names that are found in the dictionary but also by names found only in the fictionary, names that I make up and choose. Actually, everybody does it. My parents named me Margherita, but I like to be called Maga or Magic. My classmates like to poke fun, because I'm not what you would call slender, and so they call me Mega-Rita; my grandfather, who has a touch of old-timer's disease, calls me Margheritina, or sometimes Mariella, Marisella, or else Venusta, which was his sister's name. But, especially when I'm being cheerful, he calls me Margherita Dolce Vita.

The traffic cop I used to zip past on my bicycle would call me SlowDownMadge. My teachers call me HushDownThere. The first love of my life—well, actually the first and *last* love of my life—used to call me Minnie. He lived with his uncle and aunt and had a Disneyish view of life. Back then, we both had braces, and when we kissed the metal would clash like a duel in the *Iliad*. But I think back on those kisses with regret.

You can be fourteen and a half and have regrets, you know. You think I'm too young to have regrets? What if I die when I'm fifteen?

Anyway, I was talking about the stars. The strange thing is that the sky had been clear just a few minutes earlier when I took Sleepy, my dog, out for his usual walkabout of sixty mini-pees.

So it couldn't be clouds covering the stars. I opened the window and saw that right where an hour before there had been a meadow and trees they had erected a giant billboard, the size of a drive-in movie screen, about 150 feet tall, and on it was written:

MEN WORKING.

That huge board was covering the stars. What's going on? I wondered.

I poked my head out a little further, like a turtle in springtime, and I saw a huge assortment of trucks. They were unloading sheets of glass, pipes, and blocks of concrete, as well as sinks and tiles. Then it dawned on me.

We had known for a while that someone had bought the lot next door to us and was planning to build a house on it.

I was all excited. I wanted to wake Mamma or Grandpa or my brothers, but it was late, so I whistled for Sleepy, and he trotted over.

Sleepy is my catadogue, so called because he is not so much a mongrel as he is a genuine catalogue of every breed of dog and species of animal (and possibly plant) that has ever lived on planet Earth. I have to laugh when I read about experiments with DNA and cloning. Sleepy is more complicated than that. He is a genuine arcimboldo, one of nature's most mysterious contrivances. Let me try to describe him:

Cylindrical piggy body.

Front paws like a platypus.

Back paws like a froggy gone a-courting.

Right ear standing up, like a desert fox.

Left ear drooping, like a cocker spaniel.

Pterodactyl muzzle, chameleon eyes, water-buffalo nostrils, German-brewer whiskers, piranha-fish teeth.

Backside of a duck.

Twisted monkey tail.

The spotted, speckled coat of a jackalope. I'm not sure I could pinpoint the color. Let's say, the color of a mechanic's rag.

Add to the mix a sprinkling of bat, caiman, and sea-cucumber chromosomes.

And we haven't even begun to explore Sleepy's beauty.

My grandfather says that all beauty is complex, and that Sleepy is like a house, or the whole world, really. Every house has its formal livingroom, its gleaming bathroom, its antique furniture; but there is also a dusty broom closet, slimy plumbing, and woodworms gnawing away at the beams, a playroom, and a dark cellar to frighten—and attract—us kids. In every house we think we know well, there is always something forgotten, something hidden. A drawer, shut tight, with a bloody knife tucked in among the innocent spoons. In the backyard, we might find a mysterious phrase carved into the bark of a tree, or a flower we've never seen before. Along the road we walk down every day, there is a dark alley. Under the city flows a subterranean river. Somewhere in our village, a band of assassins lives in hiding.

But Sleepy isn't a metaphor. He is flesh and blood and ivory; he has feelings and memories. When he was a puppy, somebody abandoned him in a Dumpster. The sound of the lid closing like a tombstone scarred him for life. Now, whenever Sleepy hears thunder or the sound of sheet metal clanging, and especially when he hears the din of a garbage truck, his fear mummifies him. He goes as stiff as a plush toy left in the freezer, legs poking straight into the air, and there he stays, motionless, for a whole day, until he finally revives. The veterinarian calls this hysterical narcolepsy. I call it psycho-sleep-o-lepsy, and when I get my degree in medicine, I'll write my thesis on it. Would you like to learn about some of the other mysteries of my dog? Then let me tell you: he sometimes emits noiseless, treacherous farts, as foul-smelling as the breath of a sick whale that has dined on out-of-date plankton, rotten sardines, and marathon-runners' underpants. Mamma doesn't like me saying so, but it is the pure, unvarnished truth.

Sleepy came into the room wagging his tail, which is to say, unrolling his tail like a New Year's Eve noisemaker, but fortunately with none of the accompanying sound effects. I whispered to him: "Sleepy, Sleepy, we're going to have neighbors!"

I took him in my arms, despite the boggy scent, and together we gazed out upon our little fairytale world.

Our backyard, with the single fir tree that at Christmas we deck with lights and ornaments, even if no one can see it, except maybe someone looking down from a passing plane.

The swing, where my brothers would send me flying, sometimes up to the sky, sometimes down to the ground.

Our car, as dented as the face of an old boxer.

The slightly overgrown garden, with a magnolia tree, a rosemary bush, and a bed of roses, Sleepy's favorite urinal.

An authentic fake Roman amphora, the last lingering relic of my father's nouveau trailer-trash period. Last year, where it now stands, there were seven magnificent ceramic gnomes, but then Mamma read in a magazine that they were vulgar, and made my father remove them.

At the very back of the yard, you can see our childhood ship of dreams: dad's warehouse-shed, guarded by two rusty car skulls, puddles of gasoline, oil drums, car springs, and all sorts of other mechanical guts and gizzards.

Running right in front of the house is a road called the Western Ring Road, edged with stuttering streetlamps.

Across the road, billboards and a barricade of apartment buildings, all identical. The colorless and necessary outskirts of town.

Behind the house is the Great Meadow, a relic of an ancient countryside once inhabited by stables full of moo-o-saurs and chicken houses filled with skewerless chickens.

At this time of year, the meadow is covered with white and yellow daisies, poppies and dandelions; wild chicory, spear grass, and nettles grow rampant in huge disheveled thickets, and beyond the thickets you can see a row of poplars standing watch and a small trickling brook that was once a river. From the far side of the reed thicket, the highway whispers its perennial lament of hurrying traffic.

Far in the distance stands a row of smokestacks, each emitting a different-colored plume of smoke, like so many enormous magic markers.

But if you wade through the high grass, braving the stinging nettles and thorn bushes, right in the middle of the meadow, you will see the red forest, a tenacious platoon of trees that conceals the ruins of a house destroyed by bombing, with all its stories.

Here lives the ghost of the Dust Girl, my sweet and frightening friend.

Of course, one day the smokestacks will fall, the river will dry up, the highway will be abandoned, littered with the hulks of cars, skeletons clinging to the steering wheels, and daisies—maybe even my namesake, the marguerite daisies—will rule the world.

And the Dust Girl will once again be queen.

Right, Sleepy?

He looked out at the scaffolding on the house under construction, twisted out of my arms, and scurried under the bed.

Bad sign, because Sleepy is a prophet of calamity, he is a clairvoyant animal, like his cousin Julius, the hoopoe, and the ill-augured raven. According to a proverb:

If Sleepy hides under the bed,
Face the coming week with dread.

Mamma came into my room; she must have heard that I wasn't asleep yet. She understood that I was restless, and she said, "Don't worry, everything will be all right."

I said nothing. What could I say? When children grow up and become adults, they immediately understand that what they were told when they were little was not true, and yet they recycle the age-old lie to their own children. Everyone wants to hand a better world down to their children, it is a game of Chinese telephone that has been going on for centuries, and the result is this world, this tissue of hatred.

And so I, a girl past her sell-by date, believe:

a) that grown-ups have nothing left to teach us;

b) that it would probably be better if we made the decisions and they wrote classroom compositions against war;

c) that they ought to stop making movies where justice triumphs, and arrange for it to do its triumphing directly outside the exit of the movie house.

Well, okay, I admit it: I'm argumentative.

*

Oh, I forgot: every so often I like to pretend that I am an old lady, telling the story of my life to an angel, in Heaven's waiting room, or Hell's (I imagine that they will be roughly the same. After all, it's the same travel agency).

Or else I imagine that I live in a floating house in the middle of a vast swamp, and outside there is a traffic jam of motor-boats, all honking their boat horns. The world has been flooded with water, and I am telling the story of my life as a survivor to my daughter Margherana (the children in this hypothetical future of mine will be amphibious). And I will tell her: even though my life was full of surprises and odd occurrences and bolts of lightning and darkness, I felt lonely, in that unique and frightening way you feel lonely when you are a child. And yet, at the same time, I hoped that the next morning I would wake up to discover that I was a queen.

And she would ask me: what about the Dust Girl?

One day I'll tell you about her.

2. My Family

I had a dream. I dreamt that it was the spring of many years ago, almost five. I was counting because we were playing hide-and-seek, and I was "it." I was leaning against a tree and covering my eyes. I recited to myself, ten times over, the old nursery rhyme:

> *Boogeyman, boogeyman, boogeyman, boo!*
> *Is this all a game or is it true?*

Suddenly, I was afraid that if I opened my eyes, the world would be completely different, or just vanish.

And that's what happened: the big shed sifted to the ground in a pile of dust, the blades of grass in the meadow pelted up into the sky, like a rain shower in reverse, and the sun, the countryside, the horizon . . . everything fled, stampeding into the distance as I watched through the slits of my half-closed eyes.

I shook off the delirious parasites of my nocturnal existence. In other words, I woke up. I heard a succession of odd sounds, looked out the window, and wondered if I was still dreaming. Where the mole-riddled and nettle-studded meadow had stretched out only yesterday, there was now a flat fenced expanse of gravel and cement. Sticking straight up was the skeleton of a house under construction, a huge Cube bristling with scaffolding and clambering builders. Looming over it all were two hulking cranes, hoisting massive sheets of black glass and great steel beams. Overnight, the world had changed. Yesterday, we were a solitary house, amidst meadows at the edge of town; today we are an urban cluster.

Maybe we'll get a sign, like the ones you see at the city limits: Meadow Houses, or Cubic Village, or Blondie Center. That'd be for me.

Of course, I wasn't alone in my astonishment.

My dad was standing outside our front door in his pajamas, shaking his head in bafflement. My brothers stood staring, their moon-faces both eloquently blank. My big brother was scratching his butt, my little brother was scratching his crotch, but otherwise they were motionless, as if they had fallen under a spell.

Even Sleepy was there, eyeing the scene from behind a bush.

Then Mamma, hair tangled like a bad-tempered rock star, stepped out the door, shouting: "Come eat your breakfast or I swear it goes in the garbage!"

Everyone rushed inside, because no one wanted to miss one of Mamma's morning meals. We hastily took our places around the breakfast table. Steam billowed up from the mugs of coffee and hot milk, and we plunged our chosen victims into the seething fragrant liquid. Some dropped breakfast cookies in, some dipped slices of bread, some shook in corn flakes, and some (me, for instance) plopped in anything that doesn't scream.

I think at this point that the time has come to introduce my family.

My father is named Fausto; he is tall and skinny, and he is meteoropathic, meaning his moods change with the weather. He would be a good-looking man, except that his hair is thinning, and he tries to cover it up with a comb-over. He has recruited about two thousand hairs that used to live near his left ear, and he has force-marched them over to live in the desert spreading across the right hemisphere of his head. He has thus created a hairy scarf that he glues to his cranium with a massive overdose of brilliantine. When the wind blows, though, this comb-over rips loose; a long cocker-spaniel ear blossoms from my father's head, flopping down over his shoulder or fluttering in the breeze.

By profession, my father is a retiree, but also a public defender of objects. He has a big industrial shed filled with junk; he throws nothing away. He says it is wrong to say that something is old: it will certainly outlive all of us. If we throw objects out and replace them while they are still young, they suffer. So he fixes them and adjusts them and puts them back together and starts them up again. He is the only repairman for miles around who knows how to treat bicycles afflicted with pedalitis, hoarse radios, asthmatic washing machines, and impotent coffee pots. He has a magic bag of tools. He says that man was created master of the earth, but that he still lacks one fundamental necessity: a toolkit to make basic repairs on himself. Oh, my father sighs, if only we had a screwdriver that could unscrew wrongheaded ideas; if only we had a hammer to drive home good intentions; if only we had a pipe wrench to tighten hearts in everlasting love; a saw that we could use to make a clean cut with the past! But nobody has provided any of these useful tools and so, after faltering and creaking for a while, sooner or later we will all break down.

My mother is pretty religious, and she doesn't like it when he talks that way. Her name is Emma and she isn't as beautiful as when she was young, she looks a little tired—actually, to be completely accurate, she looks like a used teabag. But she has nice legs, and always smells good, exuding a fragrant aroma of coffee and bouillon cubes. She used to be a clerk in a little shop that was slaughtered and gobbled up by a supermarket, so now she stays home and works for us. She is a good housekeeper and an excellent cook. Her specialties are Melodious French Fries, Desperation Omelet, and in particular, Remembrance of Things Past Meatloaf. She recycles everything imaginable in it: yesterday's scaloppini, the ham from my school lunch, chicken feet and cheese rinds. My grandfather says that when he dies, my mother is going to lay him to rest in one of her meatloaves, false teeth and all.

Mamma Emma is good as gold, but she has an addiction. She is a tear junky, that is, she can't go for long without a good cry. She records soap operas so that she can watch them all alone late at night, blubbering like a caiman. She watches the same episodes over and over of a soap opera called "Eternal Love," about a boy and a girl who try to get married about a hundred different times, and each time they try to get married there is a new disaster even worse than the last, and in the end he is stuck in a wheelchair and she is pregnant by some other guy, but they still make it to the altar, and Mamma just collapses in a flood of tears. She has seen every episode more times than she has seen Dad's back in bed. Still, she sobs and sobs.

"I never want that which ends well to end at all," she once said.

I forgot to mention one thing: Mamma stopped smoking years ago, but she still smokes imaginary cigarettes. She always has to have an ashtray on the table to flick her imaginary ashes. If we say, Mamma, cut it out, you shouldn't smoke at the dinner table, she'll apologize and pretend to crush the cigarette out.

It does seem odd, I admit, but you get used to it.

My older brother Giacinto is eighteen, and he's like a really stupid version of me. He is big, strong, blond, and riddled with pimples; on one shoulder he has a tattoo that reads "Hooligans Forever," with the emblem of his soccer team. On the other shoulder, he wanted a tattoo saying "I Love You, Butterfly." Unfortunately, Butterfly dumped him halfway through the tattooing, and so he stopped at "I Love You, But," which could seem like, *I Love You, Butt-Head*, or *I Love You But You're Kind of a Slut* or *I Love You, But I'm Not Quite Sure*. Giacinto, whether he is happy in love or unhappy in love, eats like a cement mixer. His ecological vision of the world is a terrifying thing: I describe it as "polentopandism." That is, he would eat a panda with polenta, even if it was the last specimen of the species on earth. He is messy. His room always looks as if the local police had just searched it, without a warrant. His favorite sport is to crush cookies under his ass and scatter them in his bed. He reads only sports magazines and Victoria's Secret catalogues. He has two consuming interests in life: watching soccer on television and watching soccer at the stadium. He roots for Nacional, a loser team that unfailingly chokes during important matches; it's the same team that Dad roots for. But Dad gets upset about losing; for Giacinto, the important thing is to be loud and disorderly at the stadium, and when possible, get into a fistfight with the fans of the government team, Dynamo.

My younger brother, Erminio, also known as Heraclitus, is twelve years old, and he is a ball-busting likable little terrorist genius. He has the fastest video game finger in the West. But he is also a scientist and an inventor. He has a space all to himself in the shed for his absurd experiments. For instance, he once tried to develop a temporal inverter. He took a cuckoo clock and installed the little cuckoo bird backwards, so instead of popping out and saying "cuckoo! cuckoo!" it would just do a face plant against the back of the clock. He says that if he can only fine-tune his invention, he'll be able to get out of bed at nine and still get to school by eight. He is especially fond of our grandfather, and says that he has a telepathic connection with him. And so, in order to make Grandpa live longer, he is exploring the possibility of freezing him. But he lacks experimental subjects. He tried it once with a dead mouse, and when Mamma found it in the freezer, she wasn't sure whether she should faint or put it into a meatloaf. Heraclitus is young but apocalyptic. He thinks that the world will end in a few years, roasted like a kernel of popcorn, only to wander through space, all white and lumpy and puffy. Last of all, he is in love with his math teacher, who looks like a stork wearing eyeglasses, but that's a secret.

My grandfather Socrates is a remarkable character. He is skinny and has light-blue eyes. He has done it all: from sailor to oasis salesman, from helmet-tester to a stint wearing a sliced-cheese costume in a supermarket. He lives in our attic and leaves the house once a week to fill up on disgusting filth. He says that we are surrounded by toxins and spoiled food; he is terrified of dying of food-poisoning, so he is mithridatizing himself, slowly habituating his organism to toxins by consuming small quantities of them. He eats out-of-date yogurt, rotten cheeses, water with bleach, all sorts of glue, and he likes to mist his room with insecticide. Then he gets bad stomach cramps, and we hear him flushing frantically upstairs. It sounds like the Zambesi river. He, too, thinks that the world will come to an end, but ten years from now, and it will be frozen, drifting through space like a snowball.

Grandpa has no television and no radio, but he knows about everything that happens. He looks out the window with a spyglass. He heats his room with a woodstove and reads by candlelight. The most up-to-date thing he owns is a gramophone with a stack of old records. Every Friday night he dances tangos with a ghost, Doña Lupinda de Camarones Gutierrez, who died in 1854. Then the ghost of her husband, Don Carmelo Gutierrez, shows up, and he and Grandpa fight duels all night long and nobody gets any sleep. Anyway, even if he is a little out of control and does his shopping by placing telepathic orders with Heraclitus, he loves us all dearly, and it was he who taught me the theory of chocolate.

Then there's me, Margherita Dolce Vita. I am almost fifteen, and my hair is blond, with strangely shaped curls—let's just say that they look sort of like a fusilli farm. I have bewitching blue eyes, but I'm a little overweight. I'd like to wear a pair of those nice tight jeans that ride low and let your belly-button show, but the one time I tried, the jeans exploded while I was on the bus, and three people were injured by flying metal buttons.

There are times when I wonder if I should try going on a diet, then I decide that if I did lose weight, I'd constantly have to fret about gaining it back, whereas the way I am I don't have to worry. I do reasonably well at school, and when I grow up I'd like to become a poet. My specialty is bad poetry. Think about it: the world is full of mediocre poets, but it's hard to find truly bad poetry. Listen to this one:

> *I'm Margherita and, as you may have guessed,*
> *I weigh less in panties than I do fully dressed.*

Impressive, don't you think?

What can I add? I'm a good dancer, despite the extra pound or two and a slight heart problem. I even invent a few steps of my own, because I like to dance in a crowd but I also want to be unique.

My favorite actor is Anthony Hopkins, in *Silence of the Lambs*. I think that with a guy like that, at least you'd know right away that you need to watch your step. Mamma says that maybe I'm a little twisted. I hope so. I'd like to think that I am.

In brief, my little daughter, my adorable tadpole, that day, fifty years ago, before the world had been submerged by the great flood, your mother, Margherita, was there, having my breakfast of cookies soaked in coffee and milk when I suddenly noticed a great silence and the birds stopped singing, and then there was a dull thump. And so I said, "Daddy, Mamma, what is happening?"

"Nothing, nothing," my father replied. "They're just working on the new house."

"Let's hope they're nice people," said Mamma, puffing on a filter-tipped Virtual.

"They definitely have lots of money," said Giacinto. "And I think they're putting in a swimming pool, too."

"A swimming pool is not a character trait," said Heraclitus.

I mentioned, I think, that he's a pain in the ass.

"I hope they aren't the kind of people who throw things away," said my dad.

"I certainly hope you're not going to start rummaging through their trash first thing," Mamma admonished him sternly.

"I hope that they aren't a bunch of fucking Dynamo supporters, and that they have a foxy daughter," said Giacinto.

"I hope they're quiet," said Heraclitus.

"I hope," I said, "that they love nature and animals."

Sleepy wagged his tail in approval.

Just then, we saw a giant shadow fall outside the window, followed by a tremendous thump.

We ran outside and . . .

They had just cut down the poplar, the oldest tree in the

meadow. It was on their land, but we have always considered it partly ours, because it used to scatter its pollen in our direction, and it gave us terrible allergies. In short, it forms part of our collective medical chart.

So that's why the birds had stopped singing. I also saw that where the poplar once stood, they were putting in a hedge, or really, grass a stockade. This was not beginning well, not beginning well at all.

The poplar lay where it had fallen to earth, with the inherent forlorn sadness of any large creature that has fallen and cannot rise. There was a strange silence. Far out across the meadow, I saw a ripple of wind moving through the grass. But no wind was blowing. I looked carefully, and I saw her, the Dust Girl. She was like a wisp of smoke, and in the smoke her light-blue eyes glittered.

Every time a tree falls, or something dies in the meadow, she emerges from the rubble and comes to look.

And if she gets mad, there's no saying what might happen.

E very morning that I have to get up early to go to school, I think to myself:

Someday someone will pay, and pay dearly, for all of this.

I was bone tired, it was still dark outside. To make matters worse, there was no hot water, only a chilly thin stream of water, as stingy and cantankerous as a streamer of witch's drool. One of my ears was stopped up. I couldn't get my shoes laced. My backpack was heavy. I just had time to gulp down a handful of cookies dipped in hot milk and a slice of bread with jam and some crunchy cereal and, well, there was a poached egg, too, and my day had begun.

The school bus stopped to let me board, along with three gloomy middle school students, like little deportees being shipped off to labor camp. The sun was the color of a stale hardboiled egg. In class this morning, time dawdled, refusing to move along. It felt like each class lasted for a week. Caesar died in stop-frame slow motion, Dante had written three thousand cantos of the Divine Comedy, every river in Romania was longer than the Mississippi. In last period, we had math class. We call our math teacher Manson, and as she was explaining Pythagoras's theorem, I was nodding off, slumped over against a comfortable hypotenuse. So, to keep myself awake, I went over to sit by Baccarini, also known as La Baci-olini (or "kissing girl"). She is a high-spirited redhead. She is a short girl but has a pair of what I call cashier's tits. She keeps a diary full of little pink hearts, kissy-mouths, and sweet thoughts, and dangling from her backpack is a cluster of rag dolls and toy kitty-cats, but she's as vicious as a hyena. In our whole class, only Gasparrone—who likes to epoxy snails to the ground—can outclass her in terms of pure savagery. And it's a close finish. Moreover, La Baccarini has a fully scheduled love life that I really envy. She kisses all the boys, methodically, and then discards them like crumpled chocolate wrappers. After she broke up with poor Zagara, the class lunkhead, he tried to kill himself with an overdose of meringue pies.

To stave off boredom, she and I started assigning points to the boys in our class for looks; I assure you that we were being generous, but the average was five and a half. While we were working on this ranking, we would emit little conspiratorial giggles every so often, elbowing each other in the ribs.

Finally Manson, with an irritated expression on her face, swung her arm to point in our direction and said, "What are you doing down there in the last row, laughing?"

She pronounced the word "laughing" with the same tone of voice you might use to say "dealing drugs" or "assembling bombs."

So I stood up and said:

"Well, teacher, it's true that we were laughing, and we were laughing because, in fact, we found the subject that we were discussing to be amusing, but there was nothing life-threatening or legally actionable in our amusement. Now, it's as clear to me as to anyone else that had we been laughing loudly and uninterruptedly for the entire class period, that might well have suggested that we were being inattentive, or contemptuous, or even cheerfully moronic, but I myself find that a bit of drollery in this austere context does the heart good and therefore, necessarily, only deepens the joy of learning. As for the relationship between laughter and mathematics . . . "

She didn't let me complete my thought. She barked: "Cut-it-out-or-you-get-an-F," and luckily the bell rang.

Now really, I thought to myself, in just about every movie I have ever seen, and on TV and in all the games they make up for kids they tell us to laugh and be cheerful, so that we'll keep watching and we'll enjoy the upcoming episodes and buy all the gadgets they want to sell us. But at school, we can't laugh at all. And the lesson? We shouldn't laugh when *we* are happy, we're only supposed to laugh when *they* are happy.

I was chewing this one over on the school bus going home. In the seat in front of me, La Baciolini was engaged in scientific, long-term kissing experiments to see how long she could hold her breath, with the help of a certain Gigi Marra, the class junior Fascist; in the seat behind me, Zagara was snarling, in the grip of an apolitical jealous rage. Outside the bus windows, the city was grey and drizzly; spring was late this year, and may not arrive until sometime next winter. And so I arrived home.

Our neighbor's mansion was already finished, fully built, complete. It looked a lot like Scrooge McDuck's money vault, an immense black-glass Cube, without any visible doors or windows. It loomed twice as tall as our little house, which was reflected in the glass; the reflection made it look as if our house were bobbing in a smoked-glass aquarium. Their garden was already perfectly tended, with gravel walkways, flowerbeds, platoons of lilies in lines of six, and brand-new trees, all exactly alike. Surrounding the yard was a fenced hedge, reminiscent of the Alamo; there was a pair of steel gates. The only thing missing was a drawbridge. I looked at the buzzer and intercom, and there was a sign that read:

NO FLYERS
NO SALESMEN
BEWARE OF DOG
GATE IS ALARMED

Below that was a row of white buttons, without names. So many little headstones, marking the death of cordiality. I was curious to see more; I drew a little closer to the hedge, and I heard a snarling roar. Suddenly a gigantic black dog appeared out of nowhere; it had the face of a heavyweight boxer, and it began barking furiously at me.

"Hi there, sweetie," I said.

That seemed to catch the dog by surprise. It began to snarl and tremble, as if it were starting its motor. Now it's going to take off like a helicopter, I thought. Instead, it toddled off on its wobbly crooked legs.

As I walked into my little house, I looked up at the black-glass walls and thought: *They can see us, but we can't see them.*

Then I felt a mysterious gust of warm air that smelled of hospital.

Sleepy came trotting toward me. His face had an expression of terror that clearly meant: did you see that huge nasty dog?

"My dear Sleepy," I said to him, "the extensive range of zoological variety produces all sorts of creatures, from lovely little mongrels like you to huge pure-bred monsters like him."

Sleepy did not seem reassured.

Just then, I heard Daddy and Mamma arguing.

"You have to go tell them," she was saying.

"I'll go, I'll go," he answered.

What had happened was, in addition to the poplar, another problem had arisen with the Del Benes (this was our new neighbors' name). Apparently, my father explained, inside the

Cube there was an air conditioning system with an air purifi-
er and ozone generator, but the exhaust outlet was pointing
directly at our house, and it pumped that jet of warm, foul-
smelling air right into our dining room. Because, according to
the law of entropy, if you cool something somewhere, then it
will produce heat somewhere else, and vice versa. Your
steaming hot cappuccino is freezing an innocent parrot in
New Zealand. And so forth.

So my father would call on the mysterious occupants of the
black Cube and deliver a ringing protest.

"Now, remember," my mother was saying, "be polite, don't
start a fight right away. Maybe they are civilized people and
we can resolve everything in a friendly way."

"I'll give them a piece of my mind, you betcha," my father
was muttering under his breath.

It's never been easy to have your territory invaded, since
the days of Java man. And so my father pushed back his
comb-over and walked out the door, marched briskly over
to the neighbors' house, and pushed the button next to the
intercom. The gate in front of the Cube swung open with a
slight groan, and my father walked in. Oh lord, the dog, I
thought, but a voice yelled, "*Sitz*, Bozzo!" and the beast
froze. Then, a slab began to slide across the façade of the
Cube, like the cover of Dracula's coffin, and swallowed up
my dad.

Mamma and I sat down by the open window, feeling a little nervous and waiting for him to emerge. She sat smoking a
virtual cigarette, while I sat literally chewing my nails. Then
Heraclitus arrived, carrying a two-pound jar of Nutella and a
box of talcum powder. Grandpa's groceries. He looked at the
black Cube and said:

"Wow, cool. It's made out of a material called Vetemprax,
it's a bulletproof plastic reinforced by incorporated fiberglass

made by the Pentagon; they use it to make hangars for stealth airplanes."

"So?"

"Then maybe there's an entire, invisible stealth family inside, with invisible beds and a dangerous-to-use invisible toilet."

"Your father just went inside."

"Well, he might become invisible, too," said Heraclitus with a shrug, and went off to take Grandpa his snack.

So Mamma and I continued to sit there. Even if we didn't say so, we were beginning to get worried. Dad had already been inside the Cube for twenty minutes.

Then Giacinto came home. With his usual elegance, he dropped his backpack on the floor and burped loudly. But instead of pulling off his technostinky shoes and sprawling on the couch, he too stood gazing at the new house.

"They must be loaded with money," he said. "Though I don't see a pool. But that's a mighty nice satellite dish."

Giacinto had noticed something we had missed. On top of the Cube, slightly hidden behind a panel, there was a satellite dish so big that you could ride a bicycle around inside it, and an array of little satellite dishes around it.

"Man, those guys can even watch the African championship matches," Giacinto sighed, dreamily.

That's my brother's idea of interethnic culture.

"I hope they like books, too," I added.

When I say things like that, I don't know if I feel virtuous or stupid.

"Well, you know what?" said Giacinto. "I don't give a shit, I just hope they'll leave us alone. Why should I care about them? We've lived without neighbors for years, and here you are, the both of you, spying on them open-mouthed. What do you expect: you think they have three heads each? You're just pathetic."

He had no sooner finished his tirade than a red light flashed on over the gate, and a dark-blue car with dark-blue window glass whispered silently in.

"Christ," said Giacinto. "That's a Rolly Bahama seven-seater Limousine 6000, Ocean Sapphire model color."

"Yeah, I thought so," I said.

The Rolly Bahama Et Cetera glided past almost soundlessly, the driver's side front door swung open, and a man dressed in dark blue stepped out, walked around, and pulled open the passenger-side rear door . . . And out she stepped.

A girl with waist-length blond hair, a pair of Saran-Wrap-tight jeans, a perfect ass, an artfully revealed belly button, a diminutive black top, and red, rock-star sunglasses. I think I've covered everything. Oh wait, she also had on a pair of ankle boots with just a hint of heel. She walked across the lawn swinging her hips like a supermodel. Giacinto's mouth dangled open, and a streamer of drool ran down his sleeve.

And I, Cassandra, had already seen all and foreseen all, love and pain bound tightly together, poor Giacinto, with Eros's bow already aimed directly at one of his more prominent pimples.

"Oh, Mother," Giacinto moaned in a weak voice, craning his head out of the window like a hermit crab.

"Yes, honey," replied Mamma.

"I wasn't talking to you," said Giacinto.

I gave Mamma a look that told her to leave well enough alone. I have to admit that I had a flash of envy. Up till then, I had held the title of Miss Neighborhood. There are only three living specimens of young girls in our area: me and two thirteen-year-olds who are so cross-eyed that they seem to be sharing a single eye. Now this little blonde had shunted me down to Miss Congeniality. I comforted myself with the thought that maybe she would turn out to be intelligent and sensitive, and we would become good friends.

The little blond vamp went in and a little later my father came out. He walked as if he were in a trance. He turned to look back at the Cube. Then he looked at the dark-blue car. Then he looked at the petrified dog, Bozzo. Then he stopped to examine a lily. It was as if he had been drugged. He walked into our house and lay down on the sofa with an expression of ecstasy on his face.

"Well?" we asked.

"What luck we've had," he said. "They're so nice, so refined. He wasn't in, but his wife was there. A lovely woman, tall, elegant. She's a professional philanthropist, and she collects antique perfume bottles. She showed me one, just think, that had belonged to Louis XIV, the Sun King. She has enormous respect for old objects. I told her that I have some nineteenth-century chamber pots, and she seemed very interested. She invited me in. Their parlor is huge, it looks like an airport arrivals lounge. There's a sofa so big that we could all sleep on it together. And there are Chinese vases so tall that no one can flick ashes into them. She asked me if I wanted something to drink and I said: 'Yes please, a glass of white wine.' She buzzed somewhere else in the house, and a butler showed up. His name is Fedele. He brought a bottle of Chardonnay in an ice bucket, can you believe it? Do we even own an ice bucket?"

Well, we do have some beach pails and there's ice in the freezer, I was about to say, but he was too excited for me to interrupt.

"Then," my father went on, "the lady—her name is Lenora—told me that she was so happy to have moved here, because in the city there's too much noise and confusion, and she and her husband need calm, greenery, and nature. The house is full of artificial plants, because the glass that the walls are made of—it's called Vetemprax—filters out sunlight, but they are perfect imitations, just think, they even fool bees, though I didn't actually see any bees. Even the poplar trees in the yard are artificial; they chopped down the real one because they're allergic to the pollen. 'So are we,' I said to her. And she said to me: 'Well, imagine that, we have something in common.' Wasn't that nice of her? Then I told her about the problem of the blast of hot air on our house, and she said, 'Really? I'm so sorry, we'll point the exhaust vent in a different direction.' Then she added: 'But since we already have the system running, why don't we hook you up to it? All we would need is an extension conduit and you could have all the air hygienically bio-ionized, it's like breathing a completely different atmosphere. It's inexpensive and you'll just be so relieved in the summer. I'll send our technician over tomorrow.'"

"But dear," Mamma objected, "just like that?"

"He's only coming over to take a look," Dad cut her off abruptly. "Look, Lenora was so courteous and thoughtful. She asked about the family, and said that she wants to meet us all as soon as possible. They have a daughter, I caught just a glimpse of her as she went by, but she seems very attractive, Giacinto, maybe you would like her, and you, Margherita, at last you'll have a girlfriend. And I think they have a son; I noticed a picture on a side table."

They don't have a grandmother for Socrates, I thought. But you can't have everything.

"So is this lady really as nice as all that?" asked Mamma, with a hint of jealousy.

"She's old-fashioned, she has a frame like you rarely see anymore," Dad said dreamily. "I'm sure you'll be good friends."

"What else did you see?"

"Balls."

"Balls?"

"Balls—glass balls, wooden balls, bronze balls, everywhere. She has a collection of balls, too. And then they have a dog. A tankweiler. He is a world champion hunting dog, for hunting . . . something. But he's very well trained, and he would never attack an honest person. But he's a danger around other dogs. So the lady recommended that we put Sleepy on a chain."

"Never!" I yelled.

"Would you rather see him gnawed like a dog bone?" the sadistic Giacinto put in.

"He'd never get through that fence," I said. I was lying, of course. If Sleepy wants to, he can dig tunnels, he can bore through hedges, he can learn to pole-vault or clamber up walls like a gecko.

"In other words, that's what being good neighbors is all about," said my father. "We do something for them, they do something for us.

"For instance?"

"They're going to kill all the weeds around here. In fact, pretty soon we'll start seeing those pesky mosquitoes."

"No, Dad, please!" I said. "No pesticides in the meadow. I'll kill the mosquitoes one by one with my sandal. I'll convince them that we have second-rate blood. But don't let them spray with poisonous chemicals. Think of Grandpa."

Too late. There was a horrible smell of pyrethrum, and we saw two astronauts spraying the sea of grass. Our meadow, our pampas, the steppe of our childhood, the gay and savage territory where we played. The realm of the Dust Girl.

And as evening was falling, and a toxic dampness rose from the grass, I imagined that she was watching it all and suffering.

I remember her story just as Grandpa told it to me.

Many many years ago, in the red forest, there was a little house where a family lived: father, mother, grandfather, and three children, just like us. It was during the last days of the war. The little girl was playing in the meadow when she heard the sound of an airplane engine. She ran inside to take shelter. The bomb landed square on the house. Rescuers dug through the rubble and debris. They dug out the corpses of the whole family, except for the little girl. They dug and searched for a long time, but in vain. When they were about to give up and leave, they heard a weak little voice, singing a nursery rhyme. It was her, the little girl. She was singing the song of the last game she had played, and maybe she was trying to be heard, or was just trying to screw up her courage, buried down there. And so the rescuers began to dig and search again. For days and nights, the voice continued to sing, ever fainter. But no matter how much they dug, the rescuers found nothing.

At last the voice stopped.

A few years later, though, after the war had ended, someone was walking past the ruins of the house, overgrown with grass and brambles, and heard the little girl's voice again. They said that they had seen, in a confused sort of way, somebody walking through the trees. A little girl covered with dust, her hands bloody as if she had been digging her way out from underground, as grey as a ghost. And in that grey there gleamed her pale blue eyes, like twin jewels.

Since then, legend has it, whenever something is about to happen in the meadow, the ghost of the Dust Girl returns.

But fewer and fewer people seem to see her, and—just like a puff of dust—this story has been scattered by the breeze.

4. THE WOUNDED MEADOW

Before going to sleep, I always read for a while. That night, however, I couldn't concentrate. I kept looking out the window, and I was sorry not to see the moon with its old-womanish face, or Althazor and Carmilla and Calypso and Belle-de-Jour; all I could see was the black shape of the Cube, and a suffocating grey sky. Not a sound came from the Del Bene house.

I wasn't convinced by my father's reassuring story. Moreover, I couldn't sleep for two noisy reasons.

Heraclitus talks in his sleep and Sleepy snores.

Heraclitus mumbles out equations like

$$a : b^6 + \sqrt{25} = \textit{Kiss me, Stork Woman.}$$

Sleep unveils his passions.

Sleepy snores, on the other hand, at times with a delicate mongrel whistle, at other times, when he is upset, like an elephant with its trunk tied in a knot. Since he first saw Bozzo, he has not been sleeping well. And I had a bad taste in my mouth from the smell of the insecticide. So I went outside, dressed in my most elegant pajamas, the ones with a Gothic bunny pattern.

I decided to go explore the meadow, equipped with a flashlight and a magnifying glass.

Alas! It was like the battle of Thermopylae. I saw them all scattered before me, the dead bodies.

Grasshoppers, crickets, June bugs, stumble-bugs, bedbugs, and rocking-horse-flies. All of them dead, legs straight up in the air, and not a single mosquito among them. The mosquitoes are in the puddles, down near the stream. That's how it always seems to go: to kill a single bad guy, you wipe out a thousand that have nothing to do with it.

I was carefully inspecting, leaf-by-leaf, blade-by-blade, with my magnifying glass, and I realized that a grey and light-blue butterfly, a survivor, was fluttering around me. Maybe it was her, Polverina, the Dust Girl. Sometimes, she appears in this form. Sometimes, to scare people, she transforms herself into a huge caterpillar with human hair, or into a giant killer mantis. But this time she was a lovely delicate butterfly, and, fluttering her wings, she pointed me to a tuft of onion grass. I leaned over and saw a trembling antenna. It was a grasshopper, and it was still alive. I began to administer artificial respiration: I carefully took its rear legs and began to move them, as if it were riding a bicycle. Perhaps it worked, because after a little while it stood upright and hopped off, limping painfully. Then I saw a spider that I recognized. She was a black and yellow spider that spins her web between the reeds in the ditch; I always see her there wrapping up flies in silk cocoons. She has a full pantry and if you ask me, she sells the occasional fly to her colleagues. But she was no longer the big, ferocious predator that I used to know. Now she was all shriveled and bent, no bigger than the flies she had eaten all her life. Oh cruel fate! Oh malevolent nature! Oh unkind destiny! Oh ironic twist of events! Oh . . .

"Margherita, what on earth are you doing?" someone cried behind me.

It was Mamma. She was wearing her most elegant dressing gown, with a red-tomato and yellow-rectangle pattern, her hair in curlers. She looked like a retired clown.

"I'm counting casualties, Mamma," I answered her. "In this meadow there are no longer any life forms."

She took two nervous puffs on her Virtual.

"These Del Benes are a little too enterprising for my liking. They've only been here a day and it already seems like they're in charge."

"You're right," I said. "I don't like the way Dad has suddenly turned into an admirer. He's usually so mistrustful. That woman must be a real sorceress, maybe she poured a magic potion into his wine."

"It doesn't take much with men," Mamma sighed, flicking away her invisible cigarette.

"Mamma, be careful, you could start a fire," I said.

"Oh, you're right," she said, apologizing and crushing the grass with one foot.

"Anyway, it seems fishy to me. As the good-hearted Mary Lou says to the perfidious Vanessa in episode 107 of 'Eternal Love': 'Before you judge, always take a look for yourself.' Tomorrow, I'm going to go to their house myself."

"Good old Mamma," I said with satisfaction. I had found an ally in my suspicions.

We both went into the house. The black Cube stood there, observing us. I went back to bed, but I was still uneasy.

I embraced my teddy bear Pontius in an unobtrusively erotic manner, and in the dark I had a conversation with Polverina. She is not just my sister, she is also my guardian angel. She has often intervened in my life, she has helped more than once. Just little things, but they mattered. For instance, I was riding my bicycle once when suddenly a gust of wind blew sand into my face and I had to close my eyes and stop. Just then a car went sailing through the intersection at high speed. There would have been a terrible crash. Another time, she knocked a soccer ball that was targeting my nose into the face of La

Baciolini, whose guardian angel obviously fails to take the job seriously. And yet another time, a pot full of boiling water was about to tip off the stove, but Polverina held it poised in midair just long enough for me to dart out of the way. The pot tipped over and fell, and one of her wings must have been badly scalded; it must have been boiled and dry as a roasted chicken. And then she always stays with me while I take my electrocardiograms. She makes sure that the lines are weird but not too weird. Because I have a problem. One of my heart valves is defective, and it goes *ta-tunf* instead of *tunf-ta*. That's why I've stopped riding my bicycle, and once again, this year, I will have to forego Olympic competition. But I'm not looking for pity, even if, as Doctor Heartthrob says, one of these days we may have to do a little operation. My cardiologist says that in the future, transplants will be everyday events, and we'll be able to buy artificial hearts at the supermarket.

I don't like the idea. You'll see: rich folks will be getting a new one every year, just like with cars. And they'll have two stomachs put in, so that they can eat more, and they'll have zoom-cocks, that extend and retract just like camera lenses. Poem.

> *Sydney has a new kidney,*
> *It works as well as can be,*
> *Because it once belonged to a dog,*
> *She looks for a tree and raises one leg,*
> *Whenever she needs to pee.*

Now that's inspiration!

It was midnight by this point, and I tried to get back to sleep, but overhead I could hear my grandfather's footsteps as he danced a tango with the Spanish ghost lady. Whether or not she exists, it is a wonderful pastime for him. He dances with Doña Lupinda twice a week, and they have a high old time.

Can you fall in love with a ghost?

Or for that matter with a real person?

And what distinguishes a real person from a ghost?

Have you ever read the *Ghost Hunter's Guide* by Hector Plasma? No? Well, of course you haven't. I just made it up. You have just discovered another of my little obsessions. I make up books and then tell people that I've read them. I am so good at pretending and I mull them over at such length that by the time I am done I could probably even write them. But it's fun to fantasize, it's hard work to write. What's more, if you want to get to sleep, you have to rein in your thoughts, and getting them to lie still is difficult. It's like being in a rowboat: you stop rowing, but the swell drags you along, and you find that you've drifted onto shore, or out to sea, or who knows where. That never happens to me, because I possess a strong anchorage of self-control, and I rarely digress or drift off into daydreams or fantasies, but once Grandpa told me that, when he was a sailor, he often used to climb up to the masthead to keep watch for mermaids.

How did that story go, Grandpa? I thought, drifting in and out of sleep.

. . . My shipmates used to make fun of me, my darling Margherita, but I knew that somewhere on the globe I would find Moby Girl, the snowy-haired mermaid who would decide my fate. And so it was! During one voyage, we had set our course through the Indian Ocean, just off Cape Horn, roughly speaking a little to the west of Capri and within a few days' sail of the chilly currents of the Baltic Sea, when I sighted a very peculiar little island.

The island was shaped like the tail of a fish, and its jagged coastline was dotted with inlets and good anchorages. We landed, and the first thing that struck me was the fact that all the men were on shore, while the women were all in the water. The men were industriously gathering coconuts, and the women were diving for oysters and coral. Or else the men would sit in a circle, quietly smoking their pipe, passing it from hand to hand, while the women sat in the shallows, chattering, the lower parts of their bodies concealed beneath the water. The men folk would banquet on the dock while their women ate sushi on the wave-tossed rocks.

There can be no doubt, I thought: this is the island of mermaids. I walked into the village, where I was welcomed and greatly honored. Wreaths of flowers, roast pig, bananas, languid massages. But no matter how ingenious my stratagems, the women refused to come out of the water. They would smile, they would flirt, but whenever we invited them to dance, they would answer: *tangoinnahere*, *rumbainnahere*, which in native dialect means, come dance in the sea. And I would dance a barefoot tango among the rocks and the sea urchins, playing footsie to see if my dancing partner had two legs or a scaly tail. But it was not easy to tell. Whatever else they might have been, though, they were good dancers.

Finally, one night I went to see the village chief. I said, "Chief, let's not beat around the bush. I've figured it out. This is the island of mermaids. I promised not to tell anyone else, but please, ask them to come out of the water."

The chief of the village, who weighed about 450 pounds, began trembling with laughter like a pudding. Then he picked up his ukulele, led me down to the beach, and called out to his twelve wives: "Sing something for our guest."

I'll never forget the chorus that followed. They were as off-key as a dozen drunks, as spaghetti-stringed harps, as bent trumpets. Some of them screeched shrilly, others sang like alley cats in heat, and a few sounded just like ogres with colic.

They did a number that could have been "Summertime,"

the German national anthem, or "La Cucaracha." After a few minutes of this painful performance, I said, "Stop. Please!"

"You see?" said the chief. "This is not the island of the Sirens. The name of our island is Sumwetsumdry. And on this island there is an age-old tradition. For one week, the men do the work on dry land while the women do the water work. Then we switch chores: they cook and we fish, they iron and we wash."

"Oh my goodness," I said. "What an embarrassing mix-up."

I thanked the chief and I climbed into the dinghy to row back to the ship.

But as I was rowing out to sea, I saw a beautiful island girl with silvery hair swimming through the waves. She smiled and dove under the water. And just over the horizon, where she had disappeared into the depths, there rose sharp against the horizon a beautiful and unearthly porpoise tail. I started to row harder, but a strange warm haze began to rise, shrouding the surface, and I became weak, as if caught in a half-awake half-asleep state of confusion, and . . .

Bonk.

I fell asleep.

And then I came suddenly awake in the middle of the night. All hell had broken loose. There was a sudden deafening wave of music, reminiscent of "The Flight of the Valkyries," and the vicious tankweiler had begun galloping around our neighbors' yard, barking loudly, until a voice from the Cube stopped it cold.

"Bozzo, sleep!"

Followed by silence.

Dear angel, you are going to have to explain this one to me tomorrow morning.

The next morning, of course, I was falling-down tired. I fell asleep at the beginning of an equation for calculating a circumference and I woke up again in the middle of the French Revolution.

The teacher noticed how sleepy I looked:

"Margherita, could you repeat what I just said?"

"No, Ma'am," I answered. "Today, the lesson was so complex, detailed, and thorough that it would be impossible for me to summarize so exhaustive a body of knowledge into a few paltry phrases, on such short notice."

She fell for it!

On the school bus going home I fell asleep with my head on Zagara's shoulder. He took advantage of the situation and tried to angle in a kiss. I managed to block him at the last minute, his tongue darting in mid-air, like a chameleon.

"Sheesh," he said. "You think it's a good thing to sleep so much?"

"Actually, o great Zagara, sleeping and waking up again are the only occupations in which human beings engage in which they are neither good nor wicked. Think carefully. You can breathe deeply while firing a submachine gun, chew thoughtfully on the roasted thigh of your cousin, pee on a dog's head, and let's not even mention talking, making love, or driving a car."

"Or kissing, considering that guys just don't know how," said La Baciolini, humiliating half the class.

"Exactly. But when we're asleep we are all the same, helpless morpheonauts in the colorful maelstrom, and it doesn't count what you dream, otherwise we'd all be in jail for life. And, for that matter, it's wrong to say: *I woke up angry.* Because what really happens is that you wake up, and then, just a second later, you have fabricated all the reasons you have to be angry. And if you set your alarm so that you can go carry out a terrorist attack nice and early, well, until that alarm goes off you're as innocent as a baby."

"What about that time I talked dirty to the surgeon while I was under anesthesia and having my tonsils removed?" confessed La Baciolini.

"Acquitted," I said, and went back to sleep.

Zagara courteously woke me up at my stop with a smack on the thigh. In the yard I saw a van with "B.I. Superair" written on the side panel.

The technician was there to talk about installing the bio-ionized air conditioner. He was dressed in a pair of red overalls and he had a beard, sort of like Santa Claus, but he was young and vigorous. Mamma immediately pointed out that that he looked like Gordon, the kind and handsome veterinarian in "Eternal Love" who turns evil after staring into the eyes of a horsefly under the microscope. Mamma brushed her hair and then questioned Gordon for a long time about the benefits of the new system. The technician brought in a ladder and climbed up to tap and poke at all the ceilings in the house, explaining where he could install the vents for the bio-ionized air.

"If you like, I could have all the equipment here this week," he said. "There's a one-month trial, free of charge."

"*Free?*" exclaimed Mamma.

It's the only word in the language that she cannot resist. For years, we have been trying to keep her from finding out that dying is free of charge; she would probably kill herself on the spot.

"Really!? A month, at no charge?" she asked in a hopeful voice.

"That's not all," the technician said in a sudden baritone. "If you purchase the system, you will receive this incredible gift."

And he unfolded a color brochure illustrating the gift: a giant-screen plasma television set, six feet by three, with a satellite dish and decoder.

"Well, damn," she said, lighting up a Virtual.

"What would we do with it, Mamma?" I asked. "An idiot on TV is still just an idiot, whether he's six inches tall or six feet tall."

"Don't talk nonsense," Mamma replied.

"Ma'am, seeing things clearly matters. When you go to a concert, for instance, do you like to sit in the front row or way in the back?" asked Gordon.

"Sir," I shot back, "when a cow raises her tail, do you step away or do you get a little closer to inspect more carefully?"

I think he understood, because he smirked at me. But Mamma was bubbling over with excitement. Gordon saw it clearly, and he closed in for the kill, pulling out his secret weapon: a remote control with forty-eight buttons, a technical wonder that allowed you to adjust the temperature, the fan speed, the angle of the air stream, and even the chemical composition of the air. There was a button for pine scent.

"Of course, when the system is running, you'll need to keep your windows closed," the technician pointed out, with a promotional smile.

Mamma nodded and took a puff on her Virtual.

Mamma, I wanted to say, we have real pine trees, at the far end of the meadow. What do we need with synthetic pine farts?

But the technician was the devil himself, bent on tempta-
tion. In fact, I noticed that he had a tail. I grabbed at it. It was
a tape measure.

"Thanks, sweetie," he said.

"Don't mention it," I answered. "But be careful, you might
trip and break your back and be bedridden for the rest of
your life, trapped in your house, breathing pine-scented air."

"What a nice little girl," said Gordon. "Well, give me a call
when you've made up your minds. For the Del Benes, I'm
willing to come and install my equipment even at night."

And he winked broadly at Mamma.

Install his equipment even at night?

"Mamma," I said, "did you get the impression that that
man just made a lewd pun?"

"Margherita, don't be so suspicious, he's just a worker."

"Don't you let them cast their spells on you," I said. "Let
the Del Benes have their bio-ionized air. And did you hear
that racket last night? Are we going to have to hear about it
every time their dog has a hysterical fit?"

"You're right, you're right," said Mamma. "I'll go to talk to
them about that this evening. But first let me just take a look
at that brochure for the giant-screen TV."

Her eyes were glistening with that feverish trance that
comes over her when the opening sequence of "Eternal Love"
comes on.

"Well, they've certainly thought of everything!" she
exclaimed. "It has a freeze-image control and a zoom. Replay
and anti-glare stabilizer. It has twelve different formats! And
you can adjust all the colors on a chromotonic array. I don't
even know what that is, but it must be something wonderful!"

"Mamma, it's just a waste of money," I wanted to say.

Then I remembered that years ago I had asked for a special

coloring set with eighty-six colored pencils. What did I need with ten useless shades of purple and ravine yellow and off-white and greenbean green?

I didn't need them at all: I just liked to look at them.

And in the end I gave them to charity, so they ended up in the hands of poor children.

If you happen to see a drawing with the sea in a shade of useless purple, off-white sand, and greenbean-green beach umbrellas, it was certainly done by a poor child.

The next morning Mamma was hypnotized by the brochure. Suddenly I made a decision: if she isn't going over to ask them about that damned dog in the nighttime, then I'll go. I put on my combat hat, a Che Guevara beret, and I went over to ring the Cube's doorbell.

In the yard, the chauffeur-factotum, Fedele, was standing guard. He was walking back and forth, talking out loud to himself, and waving his hands. In the old days, when you saw someone behaving like this, you would assume they were crazy. In the twenty-first century, we all know that it's just someone with an earpiece talking on a cell phone.

I waited for him to notice me, but he didn't. He was clearly a haitzmeesh.

While I wait for him to open the gate for me, let me tell you what a haitzmeesh is.

Last year, I came back from the beach, alone, by train.

Let me confess right away: I become erotically aroused on trains, because I think that I am going to meet my true love there. I was expecting him to step into my compartment any moment. What would he look like? A young revolutionary, like Che Guevara in that famous poster? A homely little intel-lectual, sweet and depressed like the lead singer of Radio-

head? A black lesbian dressed as Batgirl? My beloved Hannibal Lecter? Or just the sexiest conductor on earth?

The conductor stepped in to punch my ticket, but he was
about as sexy as a case of the chicken pox.

Then a little boy, who had clearly entered the wrong compartment, looked at me and said, "You're not my momma."

"And you're not my true love," I answered.

Then *he* walked into the compartment. In his forties, a
crew cut, red mirrored sunglasses, dark-blue suit, greenbean-
green tie. He looked exactly like Fedele. Holding a briefcase
and a cell phone. He sat down across from me. He gave me a
chilly look. Then, in rapid sequence, he stretched out his legs
the width of the seat, lit a cigarette, flipped open his cell
phone, dialed a number, and said, "Hey, it's me . . . "

The train thundered into a tunnel, and he was cut off.

"Shit," he said.

Twenty seconds later, the train left the tunnel, he flipped
open the cell phone, and redialed.

"Hey, it's me . . . "

The train went into a tunnel again, and he was cut off
again.

"Shit," he reiterated.

This happened twelve times in just a few miles. So I decided to name him Haitzmeeshit, known to his friends as
Haitzmeesh. If I were a little more daring, I might have said
to him: Mister Haitzmeesh, I've really just met you, but allow
me to make three observations.

First, a gentleman would have asked whether I minded if
he smoked, but we'll let that pass.

Second, you're not so tall that you need to stretch out your
legs; you're of average height, and you might also spare me
the aroma of your socks, but we'll let that pass as well.

Third (and here, I would say, my patience gives way to a
sense of astonishment), I would suggest that you consider the

following fact, Mister Haitzmeesh. There are a great many tunnels between here and the city. This is evident from a number of factors: the mountainous nature of the terrain, the landscape, the numerous signs indicating the names of those very tunnels. For instance: Redrock Tunnel, 1,879 feet. But, just in case you failed to grasp these details intuitively, my good sir, experience should by now have opened your eyes to the state of things. By the tenth tunnel in a row, it may have begun to dawn on you that we are, indeed, traveling through a region abounding in tunnels. Your rage, sir, is therefore misplaced, as is your refusal to accept the harsh reality: that is, that the tunnels are real, that they are numerous along this rail line, and that inside these very real, very numerous tunnels, your phone does not work. And so, perhaps your best course of action would to be to place your cell phone in your briefcase and await, with confident serenity, either a less mountainous section of line, or the station.

And yet, to do so would be evidence of an intelligence approaching the average, and that, my dear Mister Haitzmeesh, does not seem to have been your lot in life. For, even as I speak, you have flipped open your cell phone and are redialing, while I, from my privileged position, seated facing forward as I am, can clearly see that we are quickly approaching yet another tunnel and . . .

"Can I help you, Miss?" a voice broke into my reverie.

It was Fedele Haitzmeesh.

"Is there anyone at home?"

"Only Miss Labella," Fedele answered, sadly admitting that he was not anyone.

"Thank you. May I see her?" I said.

The faithful guard pushed the buzzer and the gate swung open with its usual lament. I was about to meet my beautiful neighbor.

6. LABELLA

I walked in and stopped to examine a flowerbed full of lilies. I reached down to touch one: I recoiled in horror. They were artificial flowers, made out of plastic-covered paper. Exquisite cadavers. Then I heard the sound of music, coming from the far side of the Cube, the side we can't see from our house. It was a disco beat that went:

Tunf ta-tunf tunf ta-tunf tunf ta-tunf tunf tu-tu-tunf yeah.

The guiding concept was *Tunf. Ta* and *tu* were the underlying ideologies. *Yeah,* I can't quite place.

I crept closer, walking gingerly, and the fake grass squeaked beneath my feet. I rounded the corner of the Cube and— wonder of wonders!—there before me was a glass canopy, or a greenhouse, with a large round pond, or a small round swimming pool and . . .

. . . from a mat in a pool of sunlamp, half-naked, kneeling, turning about on her knees, there was Labella, peering at me over dark glasses.

"Hi, my name is Labella," she said, extending her dainty hand without standing up.

"My name is Margherita and I am your new neighbor," I replied.

"No, I'm your new neighbor. I moved in after you," she giggled.

She's either very intelligent or a complete idiot, I thought.

She pulled back her hair and looked around at the universe with a bored expression.

"So you didn't go to school today either?"

"There's no school today. It's Sunday."

"Oh, that's true. You know, I'm so used to skipping school during the week that I don't even realize when it's a holiday," Labella said with an enchanting smile. "Would you like something to drink? A glass of papaya juice?"

"I don't drink hard liquor in the morning," I answered. "It's very pretty here."

"If you'd like to hop into the hot tub, I can lend you a swimsuit," she said. Then she looked me over from head to foot and, more importantly, from hip to hip. "Or you could pop over to your house and get one of your own. Or would you rather ride the exercise bike? Or ten minutes of sunlamp?"

She broke off. Her cell phone had just rung, an enchanting *ta-tunf*. She stretched out on a deckchair, and began to talk, her end of the conversation punctuated with lots of okays, twisting a lock of blond hair around one enameled finger, and dangling a shapely foot. I was simultaneously fascinated, horrified, and (especially) dripping with sweat from the heat. It really seemed as if, instead of being in the dusty and depressing outskirts of town, we were at the beach. A huge poster of a tropical gulf filled one whole wall. Labella was beautiful, tanned, and without an ounce of fat. I gloomily contemplated my Doric ankles, poking out from beneath the hem of my trousers. Maybe, if I went on a diet and spent some time under the sunlamp . . .

Labella snapped shut her cell phone with a sigh, and looked down at her fingernails, delightfully painted a useless shade of purple.

"I'm sorry, Maria Rita . . . "

"Margherita," I corrected her.

"So sorry, Margherita, it slipped my mind. A friend is dropping by to pick me up. He's such a bother, but I did promise to let him take me to lunch. You know what it's like. They're always pestering."

"Oh, sure," I said.

"But if you want, you can stay for ten more minutes. Do you want to work out on the Stairmaster together?"

"Thanks, I'd rather not. I really came over to ask what happened last night. You know, the music, the dog . . . "

"Oh, yes, how embarrassing!" said Labella, her eyes growing big and round. "Daddy was going to come over and explain. You see, Bozzo is following a training program called 'Wake and Kill.' The Marines use it to train their police dogs. Every night, at three in the morning, in his stall, or in his bed, or whatever, a sound system is set to go off, playing music at full volume, and he wakes up and starts barking. This has two positive effects: first, he is always on guard, and second, the burglars hear him and stay away. We used to live in a neighborhood where alarms were going off all night long, and nobody noticed. Here, I realize it can be a little annoying. But don't worry; we've soundproofed Bozzo's stall, so the music will still wake him up and he'll still bark, but you won't hear a thing."

"But, the poor thing," I said.

"He's a guard dog, it's in his DNA," said Labella. Then she gave me the once-over and said, judiciously:

"You know, you could be cute . . . "

"What do you mean?"

"Forgive me if I speak frankly, but . . . it's as if you've done everything you could to make yourself look worse, Maristella. Those overalls, like a factory worker, and your hairdo, with all those curls . . . Oh, it won't do, it just won't do! And those clogs, absolutely not! Clogs are fine at the beach, but only at the beach, and only at certain beaches. First of all, you should lose a few pounds, it's so easy . . . aerobics and a diet. Then, a nice hairdo, just a touch of make-up, and your eyes are . . . all right . . . that is, almost pretty . . . well, anyway."

"Listen, Labella, don't go overboard."

"No, trust me," she said. "I know about these things. I used to have a girlfriend who was just as ug . . . well, who was nothing special. And in just a month, she changed her look and now she's engaged to a soccer player. Strictly farm team, but you know, you have to start from the ground up . . . "

I believe everyone should accept themselves for who they are, Labella, I wanted to reply. Instead, coward that I am, I said, "All right, if you want to give me some advice, I'll accept it. In exchange, I can recommend a few good books."

She looked at me with bovine *souplesse*.

"Did you say book?"

"Yes," I answered. "You know, those things with pieces of thin paper, and then two pieces of heavy paper at either end? Sort of like hamburgers, only rectangular, and inside lots of little words in rows? and you read them from left to right, or else from right to left, if you happen to be Japanese . . . "

"Ha ha ha," Labella laughed musically. "Of course I know what books are. Only, what I do is first I go to see the movie, then if I like it, I buy the book."

"Then I'll recommend a few movies. Bye bye."

"Bye. We'll see lots of one another, Maria Rita."

"I'm sure we will, Clarabella."

I walked out of the heated canopy, shivering in the breeze. I felt a little dizzy. Too many new things at once for a girl who lives where it's not country and it's not city. I looked at my reflection in the black glass, which made me look a little slimmer. And why not? I could change my destiny. Up till now, I could only hope to become Miss Congeniality, Miss Smile, or Miss Funny. What if one day I walk down the runway, a contestant for Miss Bombshell, or Miss Legs, or Miss Mad Furious Sex? Maybe just in the early stages of the semifinals, maybe as twentieth runner-up, but, after all, as Labella put it, you have to work from the ground up.

Anyway, I thought, maybe we'll never become friends, but she is an interesting human specimen, entirely different from me. As Grandpa always says, we need to be explorers.

I watched as a bee buzzed over to the paper lily. It landed and climbed inside, and then flew away in disgust. I make honey, not journalism, it buzzed to me as it went past. As I was leaving, I heard a snarl behind me. I turned around in fear, but the vicious dog was nowhere in sight. I could still hear the snarl, though. It was coming from behind a very realistic myrtle bush. Curled up, hidden in the foliage, Bozzo was snoring. A little nap, after the "Wake and Kill."

"Poor thing," I said aloud.

He opened one eye and snarled, for real this time. I ran away so fast that I must have lost ten milligrams.

Suddenly, a window opened in the side of the Cube. I saw both Signor and Signora Del Bene looking out the window. The window slammed shut. Then it opened, and they were both there, dancing. Then it closed again. It opened again, and I thought I saw a crowd of people. But maybe it was only a reflection. Then, the Cube turned black again. How odd!

It started raining, big reddish drops of dust. And there he was, sitting on the sidewalk, drenched and alone.

Dear Polverina, little Dust Girl, sister of mine.
Maybe I've met someone who resembles you. His name is Angelo; life is funny, isn't it? There he was, a little blond boy, his wet curls plastered to his cheek, handsome and shivering from the cold. He looked up. And I couldn't think of anything to say to him.

There was such pain in that face, a grief that I have never seen in my life, not even in a grown-up.

His eyes were light blue, but as empty as the eyes of a statue.

He was skinny, so skinny that his ankle was thinner than my wrist.

There was a red handkerchief around his neck.

His secret was bigger than mine.

The rain was soaking us both, and we stood there, allowing it to drench us.

"Hi," I said.

"Hi."

His voice was nasal, the voice of a cherub with a head-cold.

"You're the new neighbor, aren't you?"

He didn't answer. I noticed that he was shivering.

"Is there anything I can do for you?" I asked.

He stood up, splattered here and there with mud, like a real fallen angel, and did his best to dry his hair with his sleeve.

"Maybe it's time to go inside," I said wisely. "The rain doesn't seem to be letting up."

"I don't want to go home," he said in a weak voice.

I didn't ask why. I noticed that one of his eyes was a little lighter in color than the other. One clear sky, one cloudy sky.

"Do you want to come over to our house?"

"No, but if you like, we can go for a walk."

We walked along by the side of the road. A passing car sprayed a puddle at us. We reached the stoplight and the drumming rain slowed to a drizzle. We walked in silence. We were truly odd, strolling alone in the middle of the vast, boundless outskirts of town as the grey sky darkened. The streetlights began coming to life, or one did for every two that remained dark, and I decided to head in a different direction. I went down a path leading through the rain-soaked meadow; he followed behind, even though his track shoes had holes in the toes.

"If you like," I said to him, "I can take you to see something strange."

"Sure," he answered.

We looked like two young escargot hunters, or two environmental inspectors, or two idiots.

We continued to stroll across the wet grass. We were followed by a flight of tiger-striped butterflies and a peeping hare. A hypodermic syringe crunched beneath my foot. When we reached the red forest, his eyes grew wide.

"Beautiful," he said. "It seems, it seems . . . "

"It seems like the last platoon of soldiers, turning to face the army of apartment buildings marching toward them," I said.

"That's what I was going to say!" he exclaimed.

But I said it first, you goose, I would have replied, except that he was handsome and blond and sort of moribund, just the way I like them. And so, to impress him, I showed off a little botanical expertise.

"Those red trees are cherry-plums, they glisten like flames in the rain. But especially there are two old oak trees and some pines."

"And that's a horse chestnut," he said.

So he was a botanist too. The rain had stopped. We walked into the woods, and into its enchantment.

A few steps further on, and the light sank into the ground; in an instant the city and the highway were gone. A rust-colored lane, and there were the ruins of the bombed house. The realm of the Dust Girl, Polverina.

Close by the ruins, there was a clearing with a twisted elm tree and its secret, known only to a few.

I showed Angelo that, sunk deep in the wood, strangled, engulfed, embraced, there was an iron crucifix. The tree had slowly grown around it: the trunk had split and had enveloped the metal. They had almost become the same thing. There was an illegible legend on the crucifix, and once I had found a votive candle beneath it.

He was captivated.

"How ever did you find this?"

"The Gypsies showed me. This was their cemetery once, and then they abandoned it. There are lots of bones in the ground here."

"This close to the city?" he asked.

"Sure. But there are skeletons in the city, too. They are numbered and catalogued, but they are still there. My aunt Venusta is in crypt number 654."

Maybe one day I'll show you, I felt like saying. We could stop for a pizza and then head over to the crypt.

"Beautiful things and horrible things always seem to go together," I said.

"Look: my house is getting ready to eat your house. The

spiderweb is glittering between the branches, ready to kill. And Gypsies should be exterminated, they are the scum of the earth. That's what my father says. And you have heart disease, if you catch pneumonia it'll kill you."

He said all this without rancor, with a calm ferocity. But he didn't scare me. I am as much a sorceress as he is a devil.

"How did you know that I'm a little sickly?"

"We know everything," he said, laughing. "Come on, tell me the story of the dust ghost."

"Don't laugh," I said. "I've seen her, and you might meet her yourself."

"I have met plenty of ghosts," he said with a leer. "What's one more?"

"Stop bragging."

"When I was in boarding school, every night we would see the ghost of a boy who hanged himself because he got a bad grade. It scared everyone. Once it appeared to the principal and said, 'Tomorrow, I'm going to give *you* a test, teacher.' And the principal died during the night."

"Thunk! You just made that one up."

"Maybe. I like to make up horrible stories."

"I write bad poetry and the beginnings of books."

"Beginnings?"

"Just the first sentence."

"Give me an example."

One rainy spring day, the German knight Sir von Opfer-delingen rode out on horseback toward the red forest of Wartburg.

"You're a dope," he said. He sat down, astride a low branch, and started singing.

It was strange. It was like a voice from behind a door.

"What are you singing?"

"'Song to the Siren,' by Tim Buckley," he answered. "Do you know it?"

"What do I win if say yes?"

"It could become our song," he replied, looking at me diabolically.

I had a cascade of heart murmurs. But I didn't know what to say to him.

Running toward us from the black Cube were Fedele and another man, maybe the father. They were yelling and waving their arms.

"They've found me," he said, angrily. He began to swear and emitted an animal groan. Then he said a hasty goodbye to me and began walking toward the two men. I heard them yell and argue for quite some time as I ran home and the rain started drumming down again.

I was running and talking to Polverina as I ran:

I have a crush on a sad angel, a colleague of yours. Or maybe just a young boy who likes to pretend. Or a ghost. Or a vampire. Anyway, I really think I'm in love. I've never been in love before. I've only kissed a boy twice. The first time was Chubby Metalmouth, and the second time was with a classmate in junior high school, Peter Scannabissi. He was chewing a stick of American fresh-mint gum; it was like kissing a dentist's office.

But now that my lame little heart is going to have to beat to the rhythm of love, what will happen? There are three possibilities, which I will illustrate in this poem:

When love is met with hate,
You suffer and lose weight.

Treat love as a game,
Your weight will stay the same.

When love is met with love,
That's one I know nothing of.

It's bad, but maybe not bad enough. I could make it worse, by adding lines like "open your wings above me" or "you make my little sky a little bluer."

Now Heraclitus will have to download "Song to the Siren" on the school computer, or I'll beat him up.

When I'm in love, I can't stand anyone.

On the way home, I decided I must be the most highly-strung girl in the world, a darting crazed comet. But everyone else was just as agitated as I was.

Mamma had gone to see Signora Del Bene. She had fallen under her spell. Signora Lenora knew every episode of "Eternal Love" by heart! She had even let Mamma watch Robin and Mary Lou's first kiss on the plasma megascreen. It had overwhelmed her: the two giant tongues looked like a pair of dueling meatloaves, the music in Sensurround had made her heart tremble in her chest. Her world had expanded. The following evening, the Del Benes would come to our house for dinner, and Signora Del Bene had given Mamma the address of a hairdresser and beautician.

And Dad had met the father, Frido, at the bus stop, and Frido had democratically given Dad a ride in his limousine. Frido knew everything about the market for used objects; he even knew the prices of vintage jukeboxes. Frido had explained his economic theory of how to get rich, a simple and reasonably criminal theory. Signor Del Bene was three years older than my father, but he had a spectacularly thick, dark head of hair. Looking at Dad's catastrophically bald head, he mused: I know a way you could have hair like mine. It's called a progressive bio-selective transplant. Dad couldn't get the idea out of his head.

Giacinto had seen Labella up close, from various angles. His jaw was still dangling. He had rushed into the bathroom to pop a few pimples, and he came out looking he had been hit in the face by a blast of buckshot. He looked at himself in the mirror and practiced dance steps.

And what can I say about Heraclitus? He was upset too. From the Cube, a woman's sweet voice was singing "Popona's Song," the soundtrack of his beloved video game, Zelinda Four, for the moment, available only in Japan. He was trying to figure out a way to ask the Del Benes if they really owned that priceless treasure.

Last but not least, Sleepy had found one of Bozzo's turds on the meadow, and for him it was like seeing a Picasso. Eleven inches of solid material, in three curls, with a terminal left-swerving curlicue. Redolent of vitamins and sirloin. Sleepy stood gazing upon it for an hour, filled with envy and admiration. Alas, his undersized plebeian derriere would never be capable of such a masterpiece. And so he lay dozing beneath the table, dreaming of his mongrel destiny: tiny turds and dog biscuits.

In short, everyone seemed hypnotized by the novelties and unexpected treats of the black Cube, and deep down, so was I. Its spell had to be broken. I ran up to see Grandpa.

Grandpa was sitting on the bed, and he was coughing.

"Damn them," he was saying. "That bio-shittified air is killing me. Can't you smell that atom-bomb stench?"

"Sure I smell it," I answered. "They sprayed pesticide on the meadow, turning it into an entomological hecatomb. But what's the matter with you, Grandpa? You're all yellow."

"I drank a pint of gasoline," he snickered with satisfaction. "If I can get a quart in my belly, then I know they won't be able to poison me with the exhaust fumes anymore."

"But Grandpa . . ."

"I'm still in perfect shape," he said. He got to his feet and his bones made the sound of a broken pearl necklace clattering to the floor and rolling away. I heard a series of *tac* sounds, then some *tar-lac* crunches, and even some *ta-tunf*s. Then somewhere in his spinal cord a firecracker went off. Grandpa grimaced in pain but refused to give in, stood fiercely erect, and gestured to show me that everything was fine.

"Look," he said. "I'm ready for the end of the world."

He pulled open the refrigerator and inside were provisions for a month, canned foods and cheese singles and even plastic bags of frozen food, slightly odorous.

"Grandpa, what are those?"

"Frozen food. It'll keep for years."

"It'll last for years if you keep it in the freezer, but not in the fridge."

"You think?"

"I'm certain of it."

"And what else?"

"You need to thaw it out and cook it."

"So that's why that vegetable soup tasted swampy," he said.

I truly believe that by now nothing can kill him, except perhaps for human malice. He went over to the window and started scrutinizing the Cube with his old navy spyglass.

"I don't like that house without windows," he snarled. "They can see us but we can't see them. Those are folks that eat chocolate without bread, I tell you. And then, why doesn't smoke come out anywhere? How do they cook their food, how do they stay warm? Oh my heavens, look over there."

He pointed to a place far across the river, where the houses were beginning to cluster densely. Another black cube had popped up, just over an apartment house.

"You see the danger?" he said in a whisper.

"What is it, Grandpa?"

"Next to each house or group of houses, a controlling Cube. That's their plan!"

"To do what?"

"To transform us, to make us the same as them. To steal our air, our souls, our music, our savings. They're vampires," Grandpa said with a wild look in his eyes. "Don't ever forget it, Margherita. They'll stop at nothing, I tell you. But they are made of nothing. Numbers. Their hearts pump out receipts. Moloch!"

"Grandpa, don't get worked up, and don't lean out the window like that," I said. Then, in an attempt to calm him down, I tried to change the subject. "Did you dance the tango last night?"

"Yes, yes I did," Grandpa replied, his eyes growing suddenly dreamy. "Lupinda came in late, but she was more beautiful than ever. She was wearing a red velvet dress, she came walking through the wall like a queen. She was very pale, well above the average pallor, even for a ghost. She was worried, and she confided in me that her husband, Don Carmelo, has been keeping an increasingly suspicious eye on her. Ectoplasmatic jealousies are far worse than ours. But she loves me. She says that she likes her men on the young side. She's pushing 200, and she's as fresh as the scent of a rose. I wonder if you can understand. Have you ever been in love?"

"Maybe . . . I'm not sure," I answered.

"Don't lie to Grandpa, Margherita," he said decisively, taking my arm in his. "I saw you talking to the blond boy. A strange young man. Different from his parents."

"How do you know that?"

"I've been watching him through my spyglass. He eats his chocolate on bread. He reads adventure books. He plays the guitar. And he is constantly arguing with his father. But the typhoon follows him, as we sailors like to say."

"What typhoon?"

"I can't talk right now. They're spying on us," he said, placing a finger to his lips. "Beware, we are all in terrible danger. Watch them closely. Look in their eyes. They have fine clothing, nice labels, pretty wrapping paper, but they are venomous. You think I'm crazy."

"No, Grandpa. Do you still communicate telepathically with Heraclitus?"

"Every night."

"What do you talk about?"

"Equations and garter belts. But I'm not crazy. Beware of them, Margherita."

Just then, the room began to fill with smoke. The flue was stopped up. Grandpa began cursing, and then wedged his body up into the chimney. When he reemerged he was covered with soot. He opened a window and leaned out to scrutinize the roof.

"Damn them, this is their doing. Radio-controlled storks, maybe. Or a gust from that horrible exhaust. But I still have my old gun. Let's see if that damned Cube can withstand a blast of warthog-gauge buckshot pellets."

"Grandpa, calm down," I said.

He was a beautiful sight, in his underpants, leaning out the window, his skinny naked legs bluish from the cold, both fists raised against the sky. A Don Quixote of the bocce courts. Suddenly I saw him begin to reel on his feet; the pint of gasoline was triggering an intestinal rollercoaster ride.

"I need to go . . . to go and . . . think," he said, and vanished into the bathroom.

I hurried down the stairs, followed by the deafening roar of his thoughts and by an occasional groan.

My family was enjoying a leisurely moment.

Dad was reading the book *How to Become a Leader in Just Three Days*.

Mamma was watching television, saying that she'd never really noticed before how small our TV screen was.

Giacinto was scratching his butt and gazing dreamily out the window. Instead of his usual soccer jersey, he was wearing an almost clean shirt.

Heraclitus was deep in a video game, slaughtering zombies.

Sleepy was gnawing on a bone, from his favorite vintage, an amusing little 1982. He keeps them in a cool dark place, in his garden bone cellar.

Not a sound issued from the black Cube, and the graveyard owl that usually bids us a brooding goodnight had fallen silent.

But in the middle of the meadow, where it is neither city nor country, the crickets have resumed their chirping. The green stem of life was stirring, vigorous and invincible despite all the poisons and insecticides in the world.

I went up into the shelter of my little room and sat down to write beginnings of masterpieces.

The Dust Girl was sleeping, curled up deep in the heart of the fallen house. The battle had raged all day long.

Soldiers and crickets lay dead in the grass.

Up in the music room of his castle, the noble knight Sir von Opferdelinden was listening for the thousandth time to "Song to the Siren" on his litho-gramophone.

From the window, he could see the first bats on the wing.

Sir von Opfenlingen rode out on horseback into the forest of Wartburg, looked up at the lowering clouds, and heaved a deep sigh: tomorrow's dinner would be a daunting ordeal.

9. Waiting for Dinner

This morning, I had an hour off from classes. Everyone else was taking phys ed, but I have a doctor's note. I've mentioned this before: my heart goes *ta-tunf-ta* instead of *ta-ta-tunf*. It's nothing serious: my cardiologist, Dr. Heartthrob, says that one of these days we may have to do a minor operation, with perhaps a little probe or perhaps just a teeny-weeny transplant. When doctors begin to use charming diminutives of this sort, it means you've got a huge disaster barreling straight at you. Like maybe a great big mound of freshly turned earth, with a hefty headstone at the end of it, and my name engraved in nice big capital letters. Not that I'm afraid: Polverina will look out for me, and anyway I'm so full of life that I can't imagine how the death-dealing old hag could ever worm her way into my body.

So, am I afraid of dying?

Well, sometimes I am, sometimes I'm not.

To get back to my story, while the other students were knocking the volleyball back and forth in the gymnasium, I walked out of the school. The sun was a wan honey-yellow. I stepped into the café across the street; I felt like sitting and watching faces for a while. As I often do, I stuck a finger in each ear so that I could concentrate and understand just what was going on around me. I started to get a funny feeling. What was causing my sense of discomfort? What sort of secrets were those people trying to conceal as they sat in that café?

That overweight man, his forehead glistening with sweat,

pop-eyed with astonishment, sketching out his rage in mid-air with one hand. Or the little man who sat listening to his companion's speechifying, nodding in agreement and mimicking the hand gestures of the other. Or the young woman bedecked in jewelry like some modern-day Cleopatra, hissing in a low voice as she demolished someone's reputation, exuding a resentful toxin that her girlfriends drank in like a rejuvenating balm, nudging one another and winking in shared glee. Or the young man loudly fighting with his fiancée, forcing her to stare into his eyes as he berated her. The girl was biting into the flesh of one hand in an agony of shame, while the tracks of her tears lined her face. Or the tableful of friends, where a gaudily dressed young man was telling a funny story as everyone else laughed hard. Or the two boys talking excitedly, probably about sports, one of them smacking his newspaper repeatedly with one hand, while the other interrupted him in a hoarse voice.

And it was suddenly all clear.

All those gentleman and ladies and boys and girls sitting at tables in that café—*they were right, unquestionably right.* As they talked, they became more and more certain of how right they were. And their certainty about being right was built on ridicule, devastation, and scorn for other people. The more they talked, the more they were right, the more their rightness demanded its tribute of words, threats, and gestures. As that tribute piled up, all the others, those who were in the wrong, became increasingly alone and unhappy. I looked out the window, across the street, and I saw other people sitting in other cafés: *they were right, too.* This immense, single-minded rightness had split the world into two camps: those who had right on their sides (which is to say, everyone), and the others (which is to say, again, everyone).

What about me? I knew for sure that I wasn't right. What was I going to do?

I went back to school. In the classroom, storm clouds were brewing. Marra and Gasparrone had insulted Zagara, calling him a southern hillbilly and the son of a jailbird. He had lashed out at both of them, punching wildly with an improvised set of brass knuckles made out of a door handle. The three of them had been sent to the principal's office.

How many stupid battles, how many noble and just battles take place during an ordinary day in any of our lives?

These ideas were buzzing in my head, and I was beginning to wonder if I had gone crazy, but when I got home everybody there was buzzing even louder and was obviously far crazier than me. Dinner with the Del Benes was looming nearer. It was only three in the afternoon, and the table was already set. My dad, Fausto, had carefully repaired each of our creaking, collapsible chairs, and now they all stood as sound and solid as our moral values. He had carefully oiled the hinges of all the doors so that they turned silently, and he may have squeezed out a drop or two of oil onto Sleepy's butt, to keep it from squeaking. My mom had gone to the hairdresser's. Giacinto was taking a bath—hear ye! hear ye!—soaking in a tubful of perfumed mineral salts. I could hear him splashing as he sang his favorite fight song:

> We're hooligans, we'll bash your head,
> Better step aside or you're good as dead.

I went to see Heraclitus, hoping that he could cheer me up. He was sitting in the industrial shed, intently studying cosmetic astrophysics while sitting in the derelict hulk of an old refrigerator. He says that that is where he concentrates best. He says that a good idea should be like this: as vast as the chilly intergalactic space of the Universe and as specific and precise as the right flavor of ice cream. I've said it before, he is terrifying.

I sat down next to him.

"Tell me, oh wise Heraclitus, don't you think they've all lost their minds over the neighbors? I mean, it's just a dinner, don't you think?"

"I believe," said Heraclitus, his eyes still fixed on the page, "that each of us has certain hopes."

"What are your hopes?"

"I believe that house has considerable technological potential," he replied. "But I'm not going to let myself be bamboozled. What about you?"

"Me? What kind of hopes do I have?"

"You have become enamored of the male heir, of that melancholy little blond hipster who walks as if he were unraveling."

"How do you know that?"

"Elementary, my dear Daisy," Heraclitus replied, with his cunning nutria smile. "First of all, this morning you ate only one doughnut, instead of your usual three. Second point, I saw in your bedroom that you already have your black outfit, the one that makes you look ten pounds thinner, hanging ready on the clothes horse. And, third point, usually when you get home from school, there is a faint scent of salami on your breath, because you lack the willpower to resist taking a bite of Zagara's sandwich: today, however, your breath was sweet-smelling and girlish. You're already on a diet, and you've only known him for one day."

"Well, you little freak," I said, "let's make a deal. You help me to win the heart of the blond boy, and in exchange, I'll do whatever you ask."

"Would you write a love letter to my math teacher for me?"

"Done and done. Describe her."

"Tall, sensuous, bespectacled, and frosty, like a stork in fresh-fallen snow. But we'll find a chink in her armor. Every man, every woman, and every theory has a weak point."

"Even Grandpa's theory of chocolate?"

Heraclitus crossed his legs, the way he usually does when he is about to issue one of his pronouncements.

"Sure: it's a fine theory, as far as it goes, but it is incomplete. It overlooks an important point. There are considerable variations in the universe of chocolate-eaters. There are milk-chocolate liberals, bittersweet fundamentalists, white chocolate latitudinarians, and hazelnut moderates. Not to mention the Gianduia-based Jansenists and the cherry-centered Boerians."

"What about the Nutellians?"

"The Nutellians are all mere Epicureans."

"And those who drink their chocolate hot, from a mug?"

"Pure metaphysicians, unless we take into account the whipped-cream variants."

"What about me?" I asked Heraclitus.

He stopped and thought for a short interval, staring abstractedly at the ceiling.

"Grandpa says you are a Choco-Eastereggian maximalist."

I abandoned him to his sweet folly and ventured to the far end of the big shed. I edged forward along the narrow passageways lined with wardrobes and refrigerators, antique radios and hollow-eyed washing machines. A daddy long legs spider scurried over the wall, his legs extending in compass-like strides. I stumbled past plaster gnomes and my old rocking horse. The rocking horse pretended not to see me, clearly concerned that I might try to ride him again. I stretched my legs to step over the big box that contains all our Christmas tree ornaments carefully wrapped in paper. And I tiptoed past the secret oubliette. It is a trapdoor made of a big slab of iron that conceals a staircase. My dad has always warned me not to go down there. It's only a dark and dangerous cellar, he says. In any self-respecting playroom, you will find a secret doorway. I always thought that the trapdoor led to the woods, Giacinto thinks it leads to Inferno, while Heraclitus thinks it provides access to the pluriversal fifth dimension, also known as the Abyss of the Will Be-Was. Wherever it may lead, it is hidden beneath a wardrobe, and it hasn't been opened in years. Finally, I came to the forest of bicycles, dozens of bicycles, some of them worth fixing and others well beyond the realm of hope. I greeted my favorite bicycle: a hulking pink bike, known as Lady Legnano. She has one bent wheel, like something out of a surrealist painting. My dad found her and fixed her a few years ago. He hopped right on and took a ride, but as soon as he leaned her up against a wall, Lady Legnano took off under her own power and was run over by a truck. My dad immediately understood that she had suicidal tendencies, and since then, he has never let her out on her own.

I had a theory.

"If you ask me," I said to the bicycle, "you are in love."

"Well, yes," sighed Lady Legnano. "I had a man once, a college professor, for more than twenty years. I can still feel his powerful grip on my handlebars, the smell of his corduroy trousers on my seat, the sensual rhythm of his feet as he pedaled. From time to time he would ring my bell, or else he would squeeze my tires and say: 'We're low on air, aren't we, old girl?' In the wintertime, he would shine my metal parts with Brasso. In springtime, I would take him to work, and he would leave me parked in the bike rack, alongside my girlfriends. On Sundays, we would ride through the countryside together. He would lie in a meadow, reading, while I stood gazing down at him. Each evening, he would carry me up the stairs, cradled in his arms like a blushing bride, and I would sleep in his apartment, in the hallway. He was afraid of losing me."

"And then what happened?"

"And then, as time went by, I noticed that he was having more and more trouble pedaling, he was no longer as vigorous as he used to be. There were days when he didn't even notice that my tires were half deflated. He had a friend who was a complete bike nut, one of those cyclists who squeeze themselves into a silvery sheath; his friend had a racing bike who would give herself airs. This friend used to say to my man: 'You need to buy yourself a brand new bike, with a titanium frame and sixteen gears. Make it easy on yourself. Your bicycle is old and unsightly.' My lord and master would always shake his head. But one Christmas—I remember it was snowing—he left me downstairs. The next day, I saw him ride off with Ingrid."

"Ingrid?"

"An ultra light Dutch-built bicycle. She was golden colored. He even bought her two panniers, the Dutch slut. I sat rusting under the staircase, until one day your father saw me and brought me here. But I can never forget that man. I could only belong to him; I could never be anyone else's."

"But . . . he threw you out . . . like a piece of junk . . . from one day to the next."

"If you ever fall in love, you'll understand."

"Would you please shut up?" Heraclitus snapped.

I had conducted the entire conversation myself, aloud, playing both parts: when I was playing the bicycle, I used a raucous Greta Garbo-ish voice.

That industrial shed, as you will remember, was my old enchanted island of amusements and games, my magic chamber. Everybody has an island like that, even if they often forget about it. And everyone has their own favorite toy. My mom has a Pompadour doll. I have my porno teddy bear, Pontius. Giacinto has the first axe handle he ever hit anybody with. Heraclitus has his first Game Boy, which to him is like a medieval relic.

But, especially, as I made my way into that dusty gloom, I understood my dad. Each of those objects had a history, a useful, happy past. They had wrinkles and scars, just like us. They couldn't speak, but they looked at you.

I left the shed, hopping over puddles as I went. Night was falling. The Cube, reflecting the darkening hues of sunset, had a vaguely diabolical purplish cast.

I looked out at the meadow. My little sister was nowhere in sight, but shivers ran through the grass, and strange flakes were floating in the air, like so many tiny warning messages.

I looked around: it seemed as if something were missing from the panorama.

Good heavens! The rusting hulks of the two automobiles were gone. The Niña and the Pinta of our playtime, our venturesome caravels. I ran into the house.

"Daddy, Daddy!" I cried. "Someone stole our old cars!"

"No," he replied. "It was Signor Del Bene. He cleared the meadow of junk. And while he was at it, he very thoughtfully sent the tow truck over to our yard too. He helped me to understand that those rusty hulks were really just an eyesore. And dangerous, too, with all that rust."

"Dad! How could you? You used to say that rust is just like grey hair on people . . . "

"Did I ever say that?"

Just then, Mamma came in the door, with a new hairdo.

Her hair was pointing in all directions, with streaks the color of pigeon-droppings, which the hairdresser calls *highlights*. A jungle vine of hair was hanging to the left, like one of my dad's comb-overs.

She had make-up on her eyes and her cheeks were candy pink.

"How do you like me?"

"Oh, you're lovely," I answered, in a noncommittal tone of voice.

Just then, the doorbell rang.

The door opened and in came, in the following order: A round sphere of pink bubblegum, followed by Labella in a pair of distressed jeans with ripped knees and a gold knit top, with her tits just peeping out.

A billowing cloud of French perfume, *Fais-moi du mal*, and inside the cloud, Signora Lenora wearing an apricot-colored cocktail suit, false breasts, and real jewels.

Doctor Frido, a bombastic little cur with dyed hair, a synthetic smile, and a bouquet of white roses, Mamma's favorite flowers.

My blond vampire boy, alas, had not come.

Labella slurred out an elegant "ciao," popped her bubble and swallowed it, and launched herself onto the couch, followed an instant later by Giacinto.

Lenora gave me a cordial, highly scented hug and called me "little one"; then she saw Heraclitus, emitted a musical sound of delight, and said, "How darling," as if she were admiring a hamster. Heraclitus gave her a cold and very partial handshake.

Then Frido performed a genuine court ceremonial. First he drooled delicately on Mamma's hand, whispering a few words in French, then he gave my father's hand a firm clasp and grip, landing a comradely hand on his shoulder, of the sort that implies, "you old whoremonger, we meet again!" He then proceeded to tousle Heraclitus's hair—there is nothing that my little brother hates more—and then democratically launched a concession to Giacinto: "Don't get up, please, stay seated." Finally, he observed Sleepy closely and asked: "Is that a beagle-retriever?"

"No," I replied. "He's a Spiegel catalogue."

He nodded as if he understood, took my hand, and sagely pronounced: "And so here is our little Margherita."

There could be little doubt about the accuracy of that insight.

I tried to analyze his smile. It was the smile of someone who was used to believing that no one questioned him. A false, paper-thin sneer, certain of its own irresistibility. Like a comedian who uses a laugh track.

That was it: the smile with which you would respond to fake laughter.

After this first eruption of motiveless camaraderie, there was a heartfelt pause of general embarrassment. Then a hennish cackle from Labella broke the ice, and we broke up into two groups.

Mamma took Lenora for a guided tour of the house.

Giacinto and Labella curled up near the stereo. She proceeded to examine all the CDs with an expression of disgust, and finally said, "Why don't you have the Trendy Boys?"

Giacinto said, "I loaned it to a friend."

That was only the first of a long series of lies for Giacinto.

Heraclitus and Sleepy went to steal breadsticks: at our house, no breadsticks, no party.

Dad and Frido, like real men, sat down in front of the window, and Frido, with well calibrated gestures, pointed out something in the landscape that displeased him.

As usual, I sat alone.

*

There followed an interlude of convivial give-and-take.

Giacinto said to Labella: "I ripped my jeans just like you did," and she answered, in a scandalized voice; "I didn't rip these holes in my jeans, the designer designed them."

I thought so, answered Giacinto.

Signora Lenora gave her approval to the kitchen and the bathrooms, but in the family room, she heaved a sigh of disappointment.

"Emma, my dear," she said. "That's not a television set, it's a peephole, you're going to ruin your eyes!"

Mamma tried to put the best face on things by saying that we used to have a bigger set but the color didn't go with the sofa.

Most of all, though, it seemed as if our guest was sniffing around as if she were looking for something. At last she found it. She ran her finger along the edge of the radiator. Then she held it up for Mamma to see, with a sigh that conveyed just a soupçon of reproof.

"Dust! You don't know how to keep up with it either, do you? It was the first thing I noticed in this area. There's dust everywhere, in the meadow, in the air. It dirties the windows, it filters in through every crack and cranny."

Her voice tightened till it was the hissing of a serpent.

"*I hate dust.*"

"In a place like this, half on the outskirts of town, half in the countryside," Mamma said, "there's not much you can do. Dust gets everywhere."

"It won't get into my house," Lenora retorted, brusquely. Then her features relaxed and she smiled.

"Anyway, it's obvious that you keep your house neat and clean."

Mamma practically wagged her tail. Meanwhile Heraclitus and Sleepy were meandering around in disappointment: The breadsticks had been well hidden.

Giacinto was explaining the workings of a penalty kick to Labella. I heard Frido say to my father: "what do you mean, you don't own a handgun?"

And it occurred to me that I should do my part.

What if I recited a poem? I thought.

> *At parties I'm a shrinking violet,*
> *At dances I'm just a wallflower,*
> *But when they bring out the hors-d'oeuvres,*
> *That's when I turn on my star-power.*

But there was no need for poetry, things were going better now.

Mamma and Lenora began to reminisce about the episode of "Eternal Love" when Mary Lou is terrified that she has cancer, but then it turns out that the hospital had just mixed up the x-rays, and, happily, it's her mother who has the tumor.

Giacinto and Labella agreed that the MTV Awards totally rock.

Dad was explaining passionately to Frido how to repair bicycles while Frido was adding sums on a sheet of paper.

And I felt a cloud billowing up in my heart, an evil fore-shadowing.

My head started spinning, and I implored my angel-sister please, please not to let me faint, it really wasn't the right time for it. I snuck into the kitchen and swallowed a gulp of wine: it gave me new strength. I said to myself: hold on, Margheri-ta, your family needs you.

"Dinner is served," Mamma announced.

Mamma had set the table according to the directions given

in a book called *Dining with the Queen*. There were five pieces of silverware next to each dish. Unfortunately, we had forgotten to do any advance training. My dad looked at his silverware as if it were Dr. Frankenstein's scalpels. Giacinto was visibly sweating. Heraclitus, with one of his adroit moves, immediately hid three pieces of cutlery under his seat.

The menu was as follows:

The Three Musketeers Cold Cut Tray
Let-It-Cool Lasagna
Remembrance of Things Past Meatloaf
Tri Tri Cake

Let me explain the origin of the names, one dish at a time.

First of all, The Three Musketeers Cold Cut Tray was given that name because as soon as it is served, during a normal meal, everyone instantly lunges forward, forks in hand, eager to spear a slice of cold cuts before the tray is empty, and they all clash utensils in mid-air; you immediately expect someone to cry "All for one, and one for all!" Usually, the first one to get a bite of cold cuts is Porthos (Heraclitus), who snatches up the prosciutto with his fingers.

But this time we were frozen in place by our exquisite sense of etiquette: the tray arrived, in fact, two trays, and there was no ensuing thrust and parry. Even the Del Benes acted nonchalant.

There were smiles and polite little grimaces and a background noise of Giacinto's stomach snarling like a bobcat, and finally my dad screwed up his courage and said, "Signora Lenora, may I serve you?"

And he fanned a slice of prosciutto onto her plate. The whole table relaxed, and everyone started to serve themselves. Heraclitus reached out, fingers spread, but Mamma stopped him cold, mid-grasp, with a murderous glare. Heraclitus, muttering to himself, speared a slice of speck with his knife.

I saw Giacinto pass the plate of salami to Labella, and she immediately trilled: "Oh, just one slice for me, thank you."

Just one slice for me, thank you.

I have only said those words once in my life, in 2001, and I was referring to pumpkin dumplings, the only thing on earth I hate to eat, aside, perhaps, from human flesh.

After the first bolus had been gulped down, Frido began to deliver his speech: he said that he was very pleased to have such charming neighbors, because the neighborhood was much more isolated than he had expected, and there were questionable individuals lurking around, he had seen lots of graffiti on the walls and—especially worrisome—he had discovered that there was a Gypsy encampment by the river, he couldn't understand how the authorities permitted such a thing and he asked my dad if they had ever stolen anything.

"No," my dad answered.

"Are you quite sure?" Frido asked, in an inquisitorial tone of voice.

"Well, once a hammer went missing," my dad admitted.

"We should do something about this," said Frido.

I was about to point out that Gypsies do steal sometimes, but much less frequently than the residents of Monte Carlo, and some of them are quite nice, especially a boy named Darko who squeegees windshields at the intersection, but I knew that it would be better to say nothing.

"I noticed that there is a little grove of trees in the middle of the fields," Frido went on. "Just a few gnarly trees with peeling bark. I've heard that there are also the ruins of an abandoned house. Aren't you concerned that it might be used by tramps and drug addicts as a hideout? Wouldn't it be best to bulldoze it all?"

"Nobody lives in that woods," I said. "Just a ghost."

"A ghost, that's a good one," said Frido, following up with a derisive snicker. But the snicker suddenly yawned out into a gasping wheeze. Something had caught in his throat . . .

My dad, ever the attentive host, refilled his glass. Frido took a deep gulp, and felt better.

"Goodness, I don't know what I swallowed . . . "

"Maybe a little dust," I ventured.

Lenora immediately became visibly irritated.

"It certainly is a bit deserted around here," she said. "We would have liked a few stores in the neighborhood. Or a golf course."

"There are mole holes," said Heraclitus.

Everyone laughed at his supposed naïveté. They just don't know him yet, the young rattlesnake.

"And what's worse," added Labella, "half an hour just to get to school!"

"But then," I asked, "why did you move here?"

It seemed as if my question had touched some especially sensitive nerve in one of Frido's teeth, because he suddenly turned white and changed expression. But he pulled himself together quickly. I understood that he is accustomed to putting on a face that is always the opposite of what he should have by rights. Must be exhausting.

With an icebox smile, he asked Giacinto what soccer team he rooted for. Giacinto vibrated his Adam's apple, and then looked over at Labella.

"What about you?" he asked.

"I like the Dynamo club. One of the players is Kiko, and he's a hunk, though when they signed him, I was afraid he was black because of his name. Not that I'm a racist, I just prefer whites. And then I like Maldifassi; because when he hits the ball with his head, his hair flies all over the place."

"Sure, Maldifassi has a great physique," Giacinto replied.

*

You bastard, I thought. *Wait till I tell them about this down at your Nacional hooligans club.*

"And you, Margherita?" asked Frido without meeting my gaze. "I hear that you're a good student. Is it true that you read a lot?"

"Yes, it's true."

"Good girl, good girl. But don't read too many books," said Frido.

"Too many books, how? Could you give me a number?" I asked, and Mamma immediately slid a slice of salami into my mouth.

Lenora broke in with a honeyed voice: "What my husband meant to say is: besides reading, do you watch television and do all the other things that girls your age like to do?"

"Certainly, Signora," I answered. "I even had a Barbie doll when I was younger."

"Do you still have her?"

"No," I said. "Heraclitus vivisected her."

The conversation was taking an ugly turn, but luckily the Let-It-Cool Lasagna was just then served.

The reason for that name is that when Mamma puts the fragrant, steaming oven dish of lasagna on the table, she always says, *"Don't eat it right away,"* let it cool, but no one can wait, and it's just too bad for them.

Mamma's lasagna is a thermal-increment bomb. On the plate, it's nice and hot, in your mouth it's piping hot, as it slides down your threat it's scalding hot, but as soon as it reaches your stomach it is transformed into incandescent lava. It's like drinking directly from a volcano through a straw. And water doesn't help.

Frido and Dad both fell into the trap, Frido because he is inexperienced, Dad because he is a glutton.

They both turned beet-red, tomato-red, then fire-engine-red; they opened their mouths like twin trout.

Then Frido, speaking gingerly with a scalded tongue, said, "Ekth-kwith-ite wawzawn-yeh, Thignora."

Lenora, seeing that he was in trouble, poured him some wine and said, "So, Emma, for the bio-ionized air, have you made a decision?"

"Not really," said Mamma.

"Well, since we had it installed, we haven't had any problems with allergies and rheumatism," said Frido. "And then there's the bargain on that giant-screen plasma TV."

"Couldn't we get the giant-screen TV without the air?" asked Giacinto.

"I knew you'd want it!" exclaimed Frido triumphantly. "They'll deliver it tomorrow."

My father and mother looked at one another, two fish dangling from the same hook. We've fallen into a trap, I wanted to yell. But it was too late.

"You must be delighted," said dad.

"Ye-e-e-ess," said Mamma.

The Remembrance of Things Past Meatloaf was served.

This dish had a second name, the "Yesterday Meatloaf," referring to the fact that nothing in it dated back longer than the day before: nothing recycled from last month, that is.

"Delicious," said Frido.

"It's all fresh," said Mamma. "Except for a few slices of veal from last Saturday, and they really add flavor. They make fun of me because sometimes I add leftovers from the day before, or a couple of days before. But I think that a good cook should be frugal."

"Words of wisdom," said Lenora. "Labella, learn from the lady."

"Do you know how to cook, Labella?" asked my dad.

"No, but I know how to light the barbecue," said the enchanting young maiden.

"I believe," said Frido with a suave little burp, "that it's right to value old things. But for the economy to thrive, we need new things, too! For instance, Fausto, it's wonderful for you to repair bicycles and other old junk. But if everyone were like you, the bicycle factories would be forced to shut down, and then the allied industries would fold, not even to mention the distribution and sales network, and before we knew it we'd become a third-world country."

Dad looked contrite: he hadn't planned on sabotaging the nation's economy.

"Old things are fine," Frido went on. "But they need to be relaunched with new ideas. You know the pyramids in Egypt? Well, when all is said and done, what are they? Old structures with the bones of a chief executive or two inside, and an assortment of statues. But if I put some hotels, concession stands, and an airport right next to them, then I have tourism."

"Clear as day," said my dad.

"So, Fausto, you have to reposition your business. For instance, start an antiques shop with all the lovely things you have. Don't repair them! Sell them as special gift objects. An old radio that works is worthless. An old radio that doesn't work, sold as an old radio, is worth much more. It's the nostalgia effect."

"Does that mean," I broke in, "that if we kill Grandpa we can sell him?"

Nobody laughed but Heraclitus.

"What it means, my dear girl," said Frido, and I finally heard a genuine note of hostility in his voice; "is that in business, you need to be smart, and you need to figure out what other people want, but you especially need to teach others what they want."

"Dessert," Mamma broke in just in time.

The Tri Tri Cake is called that because it triples your triglyc-erides. It has more eggs than a henhouse, more butter than a dairy farm, and more cream than a cow after dancing the Charleston. Mamma was slicing the cake, and I looked down at my belly, and then over at Labella's, and said, "No, thanks."
And I composed the following poem:

> *Destiny cuts*
> *the cake of love,*
> *Three slices to some,*
> *To others, a crumb.*

Everyone was stuffing themselves with cake, but the con-versation had run aground on climate change; it was clear that clouds were rolling in, so everyone did a little something to bring back the sunshine. Labella let a shoulder-strap slip. Giacinto swallowed his slice of cake in a single gulp. Dad was about to tell a joke, but Mamma blocked him with a single icy glance. When my dad tries to tell a joke, he throws everyone within earshot into a state of anguish. He laughs while telling the story, he mixes up the characters, he interrupts himself with "sorry, I skipped a part, let me start over," he almost always forgets the punch line, or else he gets the wrong punch line, transplanting one from another joke. So every time he refrains from telling a joke, he brightens our spirits, at least those of us who know. Lenora and Frido told us the story of how they met, at a party at the American embassy. Mamma pointed out that Mary Lou and Robin in "Eternal Love" had met the same way.

"And where did you two meet?" asked Lenora.

"In a fishing supplies store," said my dad. "I was there to buy baitworms."

"How romantic," said Lenora. "And Emma, what were you doing there?"

Mamma gulped down a mouthful of cream. I understood that she was embarrassed to admit that she was a sales clerk in a fishing supplies store.

"Mamma," I said, "was a member of Greenworm, an association that defends the rights of baitworms. That is, instead of piercing them with the hook, so that they squirt all that goo everywhere, the association is in favor of gluing them to the hook. That way—"

"I get it, I get it," said Lenora.

Mamma gave me a look of gratitude; Dad, on the other hand, didn't.

"Margherita," he said, "do something, help your mother to clear the table."

After dinner, everyone started downing limoncello and shots of grappa. Only Heraclitus and I abstained, in abstemious boredom.

And Frido, the serpent, began to slither toward my poor baby brother.

"Erminio," he said, "do you like video games?"

"Some," he answered.

"And which video games do you prefer?"

"I like platformers, but if I'm feeling anxious I'll go with a Street Fighter or something like that. If I'm with friends, a football simulator is cool, but the ones I like best are fantasy and role playing games, with lots of dragons and swords and warlords and maybe a slutty princess or two."

"Erminio!" said Mamma.

"Oh, come, come, he didn't say anything wrong," Frido leapt to his defense. "You know, young man, I'm in the video game business too. I import them directly from Japan. Would you like to come over and see the new arrivals?"

"Do you have one . . . with a young boy dressed in green on the cover, holding a sword?"

"Zelinda Four, of course. It came in yesterday."

You know far too much, Doctor Frido. Something's not right. How is it you know all our desires?

"And you, Margherita, what is your favorite hobby?"

"Cross-country running," I said. "I train a lot, I run twenty miles a day, sometimes."

"Come on," said Frido, and then he stopped short.

Say it, serpent. Say that you know that I have heart disease.

"And besides cross country?"

"I like good-looking boys," I said. "By the way, why didn't your son come tonight?"

Another sore point—bull's-eye!

Lenora turned pale. Frido calmly put down his glass.

"I had hoped to talk to you about him once we were better acquainted, but now that your daughter has asked about him, I have an obligation to tell you. Angelo isn't . . . isn't a normal young man. He is mentally ill. There, I've said it."

"Please Frido, don't say that," said Lenora.

"Let me talk," said Frido with sudden violence. "We're keeping him with us because we're making one last attempt at working things out, but he belongs in a clinic. Steer clear of him. He's a rebel, he's violent, and he's dangerous."

"But he's just a boy," my mother whispered.

"You can be a very bad person, even at his age," said Labella.

"Totally," Giacinto said, who had already transformed himself from soccer hooligan to staunch moralist.

"Now, now," said Lenora, "let's not exaggerate. Angelo is a very troubled young man, but sooner or later you'll get to know him well and you will become friends."

"Let's hope so," said Frido, with his usual playback smile. "Well, here's a toast to our meeting. Next time, you're all invited to come have dinner at our house. And we'll make you . . . "

"Fausto's favorite dish," sang out Lenora, musically. "Creamed cod."

"Wonderful," said my dad. Then, he thought for a moment. "How did you know that creamed cod is my favorite dish?"

"You told me in the car, don't you remember?" said Frido. "What do you think we are, sorcerers?"

"Hmmm, maybe I did, I can't recall," said my dad, clearly a little baffled. "By the way, speaking of sorcerers, do you know the joke about the Indian sorcerer?"

"I sure do!" said Heraclitus, and ran out of the room.

"Guess what our favorite dish is," asked Frido.

"We'll know soon enough," said Giacinto with a laugh. "Grandpa spies on you all day long with his telescope."

Giacinto, you asshole, shut up.

"Oh, really?" replied Frido. "Then I'll have to make sure that I'm always wearing clean pajamas."

"And I'll have to make sure that I don't walk around the house in a thong," added Labella.

Giacinto emitted a moan, and I was afraid he was going to run to the bathroom to jerk off right then. I took Sleepy out for a walk: seventy-six minipees, a clear indication of anxiety. When I got back in, around ten o'clock, I smelled something strange. I recognized it immediately: it was the scent of a boring conversation. The Del Benes were trying to infect us with the bacteriological weapon of the century: boredom. The same weapon that makes you think that waiting to live is less work than living. So I waited for an opportune pause in the weary chit-chat, and yelled, "There's a piece of road-kill outside, a cat as flat as a pancake with its eyes close together, like a flounder!"

It wasn't true, but it was a bracing shock, and it dissolved the hypnotic trance. No one said a word to me after that, but the conversation livened up, and the topic turned to "why animals are superior to humans." I heard Mamma ask Lenora if she minded if Mamma had a virtual smoke, and Lenora laughed. She stopped laughing though when Mamma asked for a light. I heard Frido asking about Grandpa.

"Really? He goes to the supermarket on Wednesdays?"

My heart went *ta-tunf*. Sleepy came over, wagging his tail, to reassure me.

Maybe I'm getting to be a little paranoid. I walked out into the yard. I saw Angelo playing his guitar up in a window in the Cube. He seemed relaxed. I waved at him. He didn't wave back, he just kept playing his guitar. Heraclitus appeared behind me.

"He doesn't cast a shadow."

"What did you say?"

"Your sweetheart really *is* a vampire," he said. "Look, you can't see his shadow on the wall of the room. Since he's right in front of the area lamp in our yard, there should be a shadow."

"Are you joking?"

"I don't joke," said Heraclitus. "I'm not some grown-up."

They all left at midnight. My heart was beating strangely.

An airplane went overhead, in the dark, its red light winking. Perhaps my little dusty sister is afraid. I have tried to imagine so many times that instant, so many years ago, when I wasn't alive yet, and she was alive for only a few more fleeting moments. Those moments when the nursery rhyme was overwhelmed by the roar of the engine, and as she ran back to her house, the tape of her time ran out in a flash. I wish I knew if she really had been buried, in the dust, digging with her fingernails, singing to herself to keep up her courage. Or did she die right away, the sweat from her run still pearling on her forehead? I wish I knew whether one day I might not also be afraid of an airplane overhead. Or whether I shouldn't be afraid now.

Far in the distance, the smokestacks are belching yellow smoke up at the moon, the lights of the city glow feebly. A nocturnal butterfly seems to be courting the area lamp. Suddenly Sleepy has begun to howl with wolfish emphasis, and I feel hot on the outside and cold on the inside. Two Margheritas with two different microclimates.

It must have been that sip of wine, I think to myself. Looking out my window, I see that the lake of grass is being tossed by the wind, and I see the lights from the Gypsy camp. In my mind, I see a fat Gypsy woman who once followed me, saying over and over: pretty young girl, come let me read your palm. I was afraid. Maybe I have a little racist virus in my blood, or maybe we're just not built to tolerate everyone, to carry all the pieces of the world on our shoulders. But sometimes I go over and play with two Gypsy boys, Darko the squeegee boy and a friend of his with curly hair. They try to touch my ass, and I ask for information about their ethnic group. It's a genuine cultural exchange. Then we sing together. They know all the worst Italian songs. Once Darko sang a beautiful Gypsy serenade. He explained its meaning:

> *I steal the gold for you*
> *I steal the horses for you*
> *I steal the wind for you*
> *One windy night, I will come, riding my horse*
> *Carrying a gold ring*
> *to carry you off.*

But Darko never wants to sing it. He says it's just for the old people. O stars, stars, what is old and what is new? Margherita, or Grandpa who dances the tango with ghosts? The screen of the sky, or the screen of the television set that bewitches Mamma?

So, at one in the morning, when I still hadn't fallen asleep,

I got out my old teddy bear, Pontius. He's a mess, threadbare and shabby, with just one eye. He has the sinister worn-out beauty of all old toys. I held him close to my heart and then his paw began to caress me. Well, yes, I admit, gentlemen of the jury, I use Pontius for my own autoerotic practices, experimental but intense. And I'll tell you something more. We are a family of masturbators. Giacinto is the unrivalled leader, especially now that Labella lives next door. But even Heraclitus, when he was just six, used to pull on his popo like a rubber band, measuring it with a highly suspect scientific curiosity. As for my dad, one night I surprised him with his trousers unbuttoned in front of the television set, while he was watching a big fat naked lady talking dirty on the phone. Grandpa admitted to me that when he was a sailor, he would haul on his staysail, stem and stern. Sleepy goes through periods when he tries to copulate with any soft object in the house, from our legs to the cushions, and once I caught him raping Pontius. The only one I am not sure about is my mother. Once I asked her, "Mamma, did you masturbate when you were young?" She sighed and answered, "Well, to tell the truth, I never had time."

Could that be true? While I was reviewing my family's erotic predilections and ravishing Pontius, I heard a noise in the yard.

It's Angelo, I thought for a moment. He's going to come in through the window, and I'm finally going to get laid.

Instead, it was a furtive shadow. It had an odd gait that reminded me of someone. When I saw that it was trying to get into the shed, I yelled, "Daddy, is that you?"

But I knew it wasn't my dad.

Sleepy started barking furiously.

"Stop, thief!" someone yelled in the dark.

Long afloat on shipless oceans
I did all my best to smile
'Til your singing eyes and fingers
Drew me loving to your isle
And you sang:
Sail to me, sail to me
Let me enfold you
Here I am, here I am
Waiting to hold you

12. The Plot Thickens

*S*ignora Margherita sits in her rocking chair and looks out at the view around her. The city is long gone, everything is underwater. The houses are all built on little manmade islands, it rains three hundred days a year, and humanity got exactly what it deserved.

My daughter Margherana goes to school in a kayak, and she is slightly greenish from a lack of sunlight. She wants me to tell her a story. Very few people know how to tell a story, in those future years.

"Mamma," she asks me, "what happened after the dinner with the Del Benes?"

So I rewind the miles of film of my life, wrapping myself up in it as if in the coils of a snake, and at last I find that little piece of the story. I try to eliminate the excessive pain, the futility, and the unnecessary details—in any case, I know they'll come back, a little at a time.

And I begin.

It had been a week since the night of the dinner, and lots had happened.

First of all, after the night of the thief, there was a general state of alarm. I told you so, Frido said to my dad, buy yourself a handgun. He even brought over a catalogue, with all the different models and calibers, from the guns used by Pecos Bill to the one they used to kill Alien. For the moment, Dad resisted the impulse. He said that a jack handle is all he really needs, but he did sign a petition that Frido is circulating to clear out the Gypsy camp. Nearly everyone in the neighborhood has signed, even people who live miles away. The industrial shed has a new shutter, roughly comparable to the shield of Achilles. From now on, we are absolutely forbidden to go in. Dad has even decided that Sleepy doesn't measure up as a guard dog, but I pointed out that the night of the burglar, Sleepy barked long before the tankweiler, and that he has teeth too.

Dad shook his head.

My dad's forehead is now roughly the color of a chili pepper, because Frido talked him into buying a lotion to make his hair grow back. He is supposed to rub it on every morning, it stings and burns his bald pate. Not a single hair has grown, but he claims that he has noticed some improvement.

All the same, I found a brochure for toupees on his night table. The company is called New Hair, and of course Frido imports their products.

Even Mamma's head looks different now.

She's already gone to the hairdresser twice. The first time she dyed her hair aubergine, but Lenora said that it was too Sixties, and so she immediately went back to have her hair lightened. Now it's the color of smoked herring.

But the biggest change has been the damned giant-screen super-plasma Sensurround television set.

The technician, Gordon, brought it over one morning. We didn't know where to put it: it's the size of a stiff sheet, six feet by three. In the end, we moved all the easy chairs, eliminated a coffee table, and set it on the floor in front of the radiator.

But if we don't turn off the radiator, the heat might damage the screen.

So we have to decide: the health of the television set, or our own health.

It's going to be a chilly winter.

*

The giant screen has been dubbed the Manta. It has a remote control that looks like the instrument panel of an airplane. Only Mamma knows how to use it, and she uses it a lot. Since the Manta has a built-in video recorder, every night she watches old episodes of "Eternal Love" with the characters all life-sized. If she used to weep quietly, now she gushes like a broken faucet, because she notices details that she couldn't see before. For instance, Robin has bags under his eyes, Mary Lou is cross-eyed, and the evil Vanessa has big old feet. Actually, this type of screen flattens the picture so that it looks like everyone is underwater, but Mamma says that Americans actually are that way, a little flatter than we are.

As for Giacinto, I expected him to fight with Mamma to see the sports channels, but my brother has become unrecognizable.

Also in his case, the transformation began from the head. Now he is trying to be fashionable, he is always dripping with hair gel, and everywhere he goes he leaves a trail of slime, like a slug. He's covered with pimple cream and he always seems to be brushing his teeth.

But his personality has changed too.

He is less jubilant and unruly, though his stupidity has not entirely abandoned him. He has emigrated from his old country, the place I used to call Maraglistan, or Tamarroland, with its armpit-scented breezes, and its national anthem of burps. His friends used to have names like Ziggy, Spudchucker, Elvis, Skankette, and Fujiko. Now I can hear him on the phone, talking with Cornelia, Andrew, Dylan, and Ainsley. He's a fossilized hooligan in the VIP skybox, a cashmere racist, a genetic mutation of my dear old knucklehead Giacinto. A knucklehead with an American accent straight out of the perfume commercials, a bonehead. He has stopped wearing the tattered t-shirts and the scarves of the Nacional team. He has not yet consummated his act of treason, but if Labella even hinted at it, I am sure he would be ready to change sides, to join forces with the detested enemy, the fans of the government team, Dynamo.

And how is it going with Labella? Not well. In fact, badly. Worse than with Butterfly of the tattoo. Labella calls him from the yard and he arrives, tongue dangling, and drives her wherever she wants to go on his moped. They go to the cafés downtown, and he fills up on pastries and humiliation. Then she leaves him for some little dandy or other and he drives back home, alone, his tail between his spokes. Labella has told him that she could never have a boyfriend who didn't have a big motorcycle. And he, the bonehead, just sighs, watches her stroll across the lawn in shorts, and then locks himself in the bathroom, and emerges looking as if Dracula had drained his blood. In the anxious expectation that she might call him, he can never be separated from his cell phone, his little iron lung. And, finally, I have even seen him reading him a book: *How to Get Her to Say Yes*, written by an idiot on television named Vergnacchia, and I'm pretty sure the only woman *he* ever seduced came with a rubber plug and instructions on how to inflate her.

As for Heraclitus, he is in a full-blown video-game-induced trance. Frido gave him Zelinda Four, and he plays for hours and hours. He has already slaughtered three thousand ogres, dragons, goblins, skeletons, yetis, robots, and behemoths, and an unbroken stream of screams and death rattles issues from his room. Unfortunately, Frido has promised more video games, and has thus purchased his neutrality.

Good old Sleepy does his best to make friends with Bozzo. He wags his tail and sniffs through the chain link fence in a friendly way, but Bozzo snubs him, and deposits pounds of huge dog turds in his face.

And Grandpa says nothing. But he understands that something has changed. Dad and Mamma go upstairs to see him much less often, and this makes him sad. He listens to old croupy records and looks out the window at the clouds. He says that when he was a sailor, after a month of sailing, every cloud would look like a naked woman. Now, the smog censors everything. Fortunately Doña Lupinda comes to see him frequently, and she is teaching him to dance the *passacaglia*. Moreover, he is continuing his inspections with his spyglass, and he says that soon he will reveal to me the secrets of the Cube.

And have I changed? I would say not, even though I am suffering a little, because I haven't seen Angel-Devil lately, only once, from a distance. He was walking alone into town. I ran outside, but he had vanished. I bought the Tim Buckley CD and listened to "Song to the Siren" sixteen hundred times. So now I can't stand it anymore, and it no longer reminds me of him.

I don't have time for love, anyway. I need to investigate a number of new occurrences.

The first new development is that Darko has vanished, and he no longer comes to the stoplight to wash windshields.

Second development: one night I saw Fedele digging holes in the yard, and as soon as he saw that I was watching, he stopped. And I noticed that he has a slight limp, and that he hops slightly when he walks.

Just like the thief in the shed that evening.

You think I'm a little paranoid?

Then let me explain. I went to have a look in the phone book, but there is no Del Bene import-export company. And once, when Labella was complaining that things are so totally *dead* here on the outskirts of town, I asked once again: then why did you move out here? And she ran away as if I had bitten her.

And, last of all, my dad is doing mysterious work in the shed. He locks himself in with Frido and Fedele and they hold long secret meetings. One morning a truck pulled up and carted off dozens of washing machines and bicycles. Luckily, Lady Legnano had hidden behind a wardrobe.

But let's forget our sorrows! The sun is out this morning and there is no school today because—hurray!—they found lice on Gasparrone's head, and they have to disinfest the school. I have the whole day free. The first thing I did was to take Sleepy for a walk. He stopped in the middle of the grass, emitted a discreet little turd, and turned to look up at me as if to say, I'm improving, aren't I?

"Sure," I said. "One day you'll take the world title in the mongrel-weight class."

Then I wrote the letter for Heraclitus's math teacher:

Dear Miss Stork,

As long as I have known you, the area of my dreams has multiplied geometrically.

Allow me to explain with an equation: let's call a normal love A, let's call me H, and we'll call you the wonderful unknown X. Now then: H x X =12A.

To put this into non-mathematical language, what I, Heraclitus, feel for you is twelve times a normal love. You broke my heart in two, just the way that a diameter cuts through a circumference. Please inform me whether the likelihood that you might return my love is greater or less than 3/5. I would like to inform you that I am four feet eleven inches tall, and that my penis is three-and-a-half inches long, but both measurements will almost certainly increase as I grow. In the case that you do not in fact love me, I will kill myself by carving a perfectly circular hole in my head with a compass.

Your humble zero, Heraclitus.

I showed it to my brother to read. He gave it a quick perusal, and then went back to playing Zelinda. It seems as if he only cares about video games, but he is video-drugging himself to cover up his disquiet. I also noticed that he has been reading a book on tapping phones.

There's something fishy going on here.

Since nobody would listen to me, I went to knock at the Del Bene's door, as I had noticed Labella was sunbathing. She came walking toward me, swinging her hips loosely, wearing a pair of rock star sunglasses. I noticed that underneath she had a black eye.

"What happened to you?" I asked.

"Oh, nothing," she said. "A tennis ball."

We lay down on the synthetic grass: she was half naked, and I was bare-legged. I've lost five pounds, but it's not that noticeable. Labella was dejected and quiet. Then, without warning, she started laughing like a madwoman, and said, "Did you know that male whales have a penis six feet long?"

"Well, sure," I replied. "Considering the proportions."

"Have you ever had a man?" she asked with a little mischievous smile. "I mean, really had one?"

"You're asking if I'm a virgin?"

"Exactly."

"Well, let's see. First there was Chubby Metalmouth. Then there was my art teacher in junior high school. Then Luigi who worked at the gas station. Then Pontius, an odd individual. Then Darko and finally the school bus driver."

"You've slept with all of them?" asked Labella, her cute little mouth opening wide.

"No, I was just listing the ones I would have liked to do it with, but like hell I did."

"So, you're a virgin."

"Pure as a lily under a bell jar in a bank vault in the Antarctic wilderness. What about you?"

"Can you keep a secret?"

"I swear."

"Well, if I told you who I've slept with, you wouldn't believe it. Just guess; say a name."

"Anthony Hopkins."

"Are you kidding?"

"Kiko, the player on the Dynamo team."

"Are you kidding?"

"Giacinto?"

"Are you crazy?"

"Then with who?"

"With Pataffa."

"Who's that?

"Oh, you really don't know anything, do you? What good does it do you to read all those books if you don't know who Sting Pataffa is? Do you know the band, the Kloneboys?"

"The singers?"

"Singers, dancers, rappers, hip-hoppers, they're just incredible! Well, he's the tall one, blond, with sideburns and the diamond earring. We went to one of their concerts, and then to the party afterwards, because my father imports electric guitars, too. Well, you can imagine what happened."

"Everything?"

"Everything and more."

I tried to imagine the "more" part. In my mind I saw a bed with Labella, Pataffa, and Pontius in sexy underwear, all rolling around intertwined.

"You lucky little slut," I sighed. "So now are you going steady?"

"My dear girl," laughed Labella, "that's not how things work. He goes from one concert to the next, he's a star, they

even give him free clothing. Every so often, he sends me a little text message. But I don't answer him. For me, it was just
another affair, like any other."

"That's not true."

"Why do you say it's not true?"

"Because you're moving your foot. Your foot is like a dog's
tail. It betrays your feelings. It means you have a crush on
him."

"You nasty shit," said Labella, turning into a baby harpy.
"You think I can fall in love so easily?"

"What would be so bad about that?"

"Well, I want to have fun," she said. "And I don't give a
damn about Pataffa. Boys stand in line for me. And tell that
loser of a brother of yours to stop sending me text messages
of love; he's ugly, he's gross, and his breath is sickly sweet."

"That's mallow-flavored toothpaste. He's going to develop
toxic-toothpaste syndrome because of you. He even bought a
bottle of My Macho scent and he's been trimming his nose
hair."

"Too bad for him."

"Okay, now you need to just cut it out, you stuck-up
thing."

"And you, you fat thing, stay clear of my brother."

"Labella," I said to her very calmly, "did you know that my
fat-girl physique can have certain advantages?"

"Like what?"

"Well, for instance, since I'm fairly brawny, I could grab
you by your lovely blond hair, hold you tight, and punch you
hard and repeatedly in that pretty little tummy of yours, then
crush that little turned-up nose between thumb and forefin-
ger until you have just a single nostril so that you'll have to get
plastic surgery and undergo ten different operations, and
even then you'll only be able to pose for calendars with your
back turned. And last of all, I would take the biggest, glossi-

est fashion magazine that you own, roll it up tight, and—to use a subtle metaphor—I would shove it up your ass."

"Have you lost your mind?" said Labella. "If you don't watch out, I'll call Fedele."

"You just call him, and tell him that he can stop sneaking around our backyard at night."

I knew that I'd gone too far.

But Labella surprised me. She unfurled a great big smile and whispered, sweetly, "Oh, you're right, I apologize, that was rude of me. But sometimes your brother can kind of drive me crazy. And then, I'm having my period. Listen, the next time there's a Kloneboys concert, we can go together. Maybe you could go to bed with Bondy, the drummer; he has a great body."

"Well, I'd like that," I said.

She walked me back across the lawn with a slightly treacherous smile. She was walking behind me. I thought I heard a whistle as the gate was opening. I turned around and Bozzo was running behind me, lunging to the charge. He was about to leap and bite when Labella yelled, "Bozzo, *sitz!*"

Just in the nick of time. His teeth were a centimeter from my rump.

"Goodness," said Labella. "If I hadn't stopped him in time, he would have ripped you to shreds. I wonder what got into him."

I did not like this; I did not like this at all.

Returning home, I walked across the meadow. The flowers smelled sweetly, each according to its species. I watched the busy throngs of bees, and the cabbage butterflies, and the gymnastic performances of the grasshoppers. One grasshopper jumped so high that I wished I had had a judge's card so

I could hold up a ten. I sniffed the scents, and behind me I heard light footsteps. It's nice when someone follows you and it's not scary. Then I heard a noise; it sounded like a tiny groan.

She worries about me, my little sister, who occasionally forgets her own sad story to worry herself with mine.

13. The Return of the Vampire

"**I**'m home," I called out as I opened the front door. No big entrance was ever so roundly ignored.

The situation was deteriorating at a quickening clip. Mamma was seated in front of the megascreen, zapping back and forth among four programs, in each of which six people were talking at once, for a grand total of twenty-four overlapping voices. She was leaping from one channel to the next, half her face wearing an expression of anguish, the other half a sneering, leering grin. She was unrecognizable. She was in a state of partial collapse because she had been forced to give up her favorite drugs: her Virtual cigarettes and her green stamps.

Lenora had been up to her usual tricks; she persuaded Mamma that pretending to smoke is not elegant, that it is a neurotic tic. Mamma had finally given it up, but she was suffering. This is the only case on earth of someone being forced to stop not-smoking without smoking and feeling bad because they can't smoke, even though they don't smoke in the first place.

However, what was worse—much worse—was her decision to stop collecting green stamps. Once, at the supermarket, while they were standing in line to check out, Lenora said to her, "My God, how vulgar these green stamps are!"

Mamma turned white.

She loves green stamps, she has been collecting them for years. She has won electric cheese-graters, battery-powered

juicers, cherry-pitters, and potato-waxers. Whenever she buys
anything, she asks greedily if they give green stamps. Legend
has it that at Aunt Venusta's funeral, she managed to get two
green stamps for a discount on Grandpa's upcoming funeral.

By now, Lenora has enslaved her completely. Mamma's
thrown away all her green stamps. And to think it would only
have taken another three thousand points to win a duck-
doorstopper. Now Mamma is doing special anti-wrinkle exer-
cises to tone up her facial muscles. The exercise consists of
repeatedly pursing her lips, as if trying to kiss someone while
they're running away.

I'm not alone in noticing these changes. My dad is irritated
and upset. He lashes out at her, saying that since they installed
the giant-screen television, she never sets foot in the kitchen,
and now that she's stopped collecting green stamps, her grocery shopping lacks passion. He's changing too, though. He
spends hours in front of the mirror, monitoring the growth of
his budding hair crop. He bought himself a greenbean-green
jacket. Most worrisome of all: he has stopped fixing things.
One of our window blinds broke, and there it sits. There was
a time at our house when a faucet couldn't drip a drop without him rushing to strangle the flow. Now the toilet just gur-
gles feebly instead of flushing vigorously, and two light bulbs
have burned out. But he has other things on his mind. He
bustles in and out of the shed, busily intent on mysterious
tasks.

Giacinto has sunk into a swamp of love and hair-gel. He's
had one ear pierced, and he wears a tiny diamond stud,
Pataffa style. He sends an endless stream of SMS text messages to Labella, and she never answers. He still watches TV,
but not soccer. Now he only watches the commercials.

Do you see why? Because in his mind, Labella comes
from the world of advertising. The world of cars that bring
you happiness, low-alcohol beverages that make you a low-

cool hipster, and video cell-phones to find your kindred spirit.

"Giacinto," I told him, "the real lie that advertising tells is not so much in what it shows, but in what it leaves out. Just think of a television commercial where the car starts out driving along empty, tree-lined roads, and then the landscape starts to change, the car gets stuck in a traffic jam, the lithe cat-woman at the wheel leans out the window, shrieking rudely in an argument over a parking spot. Then she accelerates, swearing, and crashes into a bridge abutment. Or else, imagine a commercial where a guy gulps down his tenth low-alcohol beverage, and then vomits for thirty seconds into the camera lens, with a merry jingle going *ta-tunf* in the background. Or a happy couple buy a video cell-phone to send each other messages on a Caribbean beach, but then they don't have enough money left over to go to the Caribbean, and they end up sending each other pictures of their asses, from one room to the other."

He looked as if he was listening to me. One to zero in my favor.

"Maybe you're right," he answered. "But to me, you look like an advertisement for Get a Life International."

One-all.

What about young Heraclitus? He's grown moody, and he spends most of his time in his room. The old television set has become his personal video-arena; he is challenging the Great BioDragon; you can hear the din of combat. This is the twelfth time that he's taken him on; the BioDragon always rips him a new one, but he refuses to give up.

Grandpa's not here. He's gone to the supermarket to flirt with shopgirls and to stock up on a new supply of canned goods and toxins.

Sleepy is snoring, dreaming that he's a Saint Bernard.

I feel lonely.

So I decide to go see my friend Darko at the Gypsy camp. I wonder why I haven't seen him at the stoplight recently. I am a little frightened, because night is falling as I set out across the suburban tundra. The tiny stinging gnats are taking bites out of my flesh, and the nettles are pricking my legs, but there is a nice scent of mint in the air, and the daisies all bow to me as I pass by; I may be stepping on one or two as I go.

I compose the following poem:

HE LOVES ME, HE LOVES ME NOT

If love is driving you crazy
and there are doubts you wish to settle,
make sure that you pick a daisy
that only has one petal.

I walk and walk, and the sea of grass seems boundless. It feels like when, at the beach, you swim out too far, and you can't say whether you'll be able to make it back to shore. But I keep on walking. Behind me, I hear the sound of light footsteps.

I turn suddenly, but Polverina is too sly for that. She has already transformed herself into two bunny ears, peering out at me from the grass.

Perhaps it really is better for me not to see her: according to legend, whoever touches the ghost of Dust Girl or looks into her eyes will be flooded with all her pain and grief, and will immediately go insane.

I continued to walk, and now it was almost dark. By this point, I should at least be seeing the lights of the trailers in the Gypsy camp.

But when I walked into the clearing, there was no one there.

They had all cleared out. There were empty tires, bags of garbage, a fire-charred trailer. Vanished, from one day to the next.

I heard footsteps behind me. These were different.

"Who are you looking for, Gypsy girl?" said a mocking voice.

I turned around. It was Angelo. He was dressed in a loose smock-like shirt several sizes too big for him; it really did look like a cherub's tunic. His face was pale; he wore his red bandanna around his neck. He wasn't quite as handsome as I remembered, but I remembered him as stunningly handsome, so he was still handsome.

He walked toward me, a blade of grass clenched between his teeth.

"They're gone. In fact, they've been evicted." And he waved his hand. "When my dad wants something, he gets it. The police cleared them out this morning. And your pal Darko has been missing for a week."

I felt a knot in my throat.

"Does that make you happy?" I asked. "You're as much of a racist as your father. Do you feel a little safer now, inside your fortified Cube?"

Angelo looked at his feet.

"Let's go to the tree with the cross," he said.

"No, you go there on your own."

"Please," he said. "I need to talk to you."

We walked along, a few yards apart, while the lights of the city blinked on a few at a time. A magpie flew around and over us. The last rays of the setting sun made my blond hair gleam. I must have been gorgeous from a distance. At this time of night, the meadow is not going to sleep; in fact, it is teeming with new life. Tiny creatures swim through it, the crickets begin to tune their fiddles, and the moths ready themselves for their suicide missions. The earthworms dance.

We reached the clearing. Angelo walked over to the tree and reached out to touch it, fascinated.

"I've come here a lot in the last few days," he said. "Do you know why?"

"How would I know?" I answered, still irritated. "Maybe you wanted to meet Dust Girl?"

"I don't believe in that story. What I like is the idea that this is a forgotten cemetery. I'm drawn here by this old cross. And the tree that continues to grow around it. They've become friends, one resisting and the other consuming. We should be both things at the same time."

"You mean life and death, light and shadow? That's an old refrain, you hear it from all the poets and philosophers. It's in every Kung Fu movie."

"Maybe it is a cliché," he whispered. "But when you walk past the ruins of that house, you try to imagine how it used to be, don't you? And you shiver, don't you? What goes through your head, what do you imagine?"

"I imagine that I'm running," I replied. "And there's a shadow of an airplane over my head."

"And you sing a lullaby . . . "

"Don't!" I said in fright. "You should never sing the lullaby of Dust Girl. It's bad luck."

"But I know it by heart. Here, let me recite it for you:

> You at peace, and me at war
> But now it's time to switch
> You beneath the earthen floor
> And I'll come out to play."

"You think it's funny to play around with this sort of thing?" I asked sternly. "If you make fun of those who have suffered, it means you haven't suffered enough yourself."

He grabbed me by one arm, so hard that it scared me. His eyes grew dark.

"You think you can say whatever you want, don't you, Margherita? Just because your heart's a little wacky. Listen, I'm wacky from head to foot. I'm not afraid of a lullaby, I'm afraid of doctor's reports. I am afraid of being locked up in a mental clinic again, of being buried alive in there."

"Forgive me," I said. "It's just that you're . . . "

"I'm too many things at the same time," said Angelo, and laughed loudly. "Or maybe I'm just a spoiled young schizophrenic. Death and life, shadow and light, and all that crap."

"Fine. Let's talk about light. Tell me . . . about the most beautiful moment of your life."

He looked at me as if I had said something unbelievable. His lighter-colored eye almost seemed to glow. Then he told me a story, without looking into my eyes, his hands trembling slightly.

"When I was in boarding school, there was an old man there named Ivan, a sort of janitor who did odd jobs. He looked like an Indian, and he was the only person there who always smiled and never raised his voice. He would wash the floors, as cheerful as if he was painting a picture. Once I snuck down into the basement. It was against the rules, but I wanted to hide from everyone else and have a little time to myself. In a dark corridor, lined with crates and bottles, I heard someone singing. It was Ivan, he lived down there. His voice was coming from behind a translucent glass door, there was a light on. Maybe it was a bathroom. The song was very sad and very pretty, and it was in some language I couldn't recognize. The sound of water made me think that he was singing on the shore of a distant sea. I stayed there listening to him for a long, long time. I imagined he was my father, the father I wish I had had, or maybe a sailor uncle who would take me away from there. I thought that I could have been him and all the memories of his life. That poor old man, so courteous to everyone, with his secret grief that he sang in solitude. It was a song of lost love. It was a song for a siren."

I looked at Angelo, and his strange tremor. I wanted to reach out and hug him, but he was incredibly, wonderfully distant.

He turned toward me, as if he had just awakened from a dream.

"That was a long time ago, exactly seven years ago, in fact. I was ten years old."

"You're seventeen? You're decrepit!"

"Decrepit and tired," said Angelo, and stretched out on the grass. It was only then that I realized he was barefoot.

We sat down side by side. My elbow touched his. Oh, erotic contact. This was definitely better than Pontius. The landscape around us was beautiful, like an old man's face. The ruins of the abandoned house, the gnarled trees. In the distance, the river with its thousand channels, the old road and the new high-speed ring road, the grass that continued to cover the earth, filling every crack and climbing over every stone, the poppies and the sunflowers that were daring the breeze. And every leaf was a different color.

"Did you know," I asked, "that the Indians in Amazonia have fifty different words for the color green?"

"And you envy them?" he asked, imitating his father's voice. "Would you rather live on fried monkey meat, just so that you could learn fifty new words?"

"Oh, Frido, you don't understand a thing," I said, imitating Lenora's haughty voice. "In a boutique, the right color is fundamental."

"Bah!" Angelo said. "Once my parents gave me a coloring case with eighty-six pencils, all in different colors. Who would be so stupid as to want a present like that?"

"I couldn't say," I mumbled.

"Then I said to myself: there are lots of pencils in this case, but there are so many more colors in the world."

"You want to see who can name the most kinds of green?"

"Okay. Apple green, mold green, emerald green, lizard green."

"Pea green, beryl green, grasshopper green, nettle green."

"Olive green, sea green, dark green."

"Rotten-fruit green, mint green, bile green."

"Off-green, light green, Irish-rugby-jersey green."

"Lime green, putting green, Martian's fart green."

"Guacamole green, how-green-was-my-valley green, stop-light green."

"Mackerel-back green, manger-moss green, anaconda green."

"Mouthwash green."

"Spinach-puke green."

"Algae green."

"Von Ofterverdligen green."

"Enough-I'm-fucking-bored-of-this-game green."

"But it's a great game," I said.

"It's a stupid game, and it's depressing me," he replied.

"Why?"

"When I was in the clinic, all everyone did was to repeat the same thing all day long. Streamers of words. Hours and hours, each identical to the one before."

"Come on, don't go pulling the dark, cursed angel routine. Not now."

He stood up, and suddenly his face was hard.

"You think I'm just acting? I've been put in a clinic ten, maybe twelve times. I can't even remember. For my family, it's the easiest solution. Other kids get grounded, I go into a clinic."

"Why is that?"

"Because I'm not like them. Because I know their secrets," Angelo said. "You know nothing about us. You don't even know why we came here."

"I have my suspicions. Are you vampires?"

"Maybe," he answered. "But don't investigate. You would meet an unpleasant fate, like Darko. The next one to vanish is going to be the old farmer, the one with the shack down by the river. Every word I say, of course, is nothing more than the ravings of a lunatic, and you should pay it no mind."

If you meet an angel, you will have not peace, but a fever.

I got up, and he walked along beside me.

"I know perfectly well that something strange is going on," I said calmly. "You know everything about us: what we like to eat, our favorite soap operas and video games. Maybe you even know what medicine I am taking for my rattletrap little heart. But I don't understand why you're so interested in us. Why you sent Fedele to pretend to be a burglar. And especially why you don't cast a shadow in the window."

He looked at me with his eyes of unmatched blue. I was filled with fear, or perhaps desire, that he would sink his teeth into my neck, the young vampire.

"The reason I cast no shadow is that what you see isn't a window. It's a television screen. We transmit pictures of a happy family to the exterior, while inside we're pounding one another to death."

"Are you joking?"

"Of course," Angelo laughed. "We're an average family, just like yours. Averagely racist, averagely apathetic, averagely greedy. But the worst one of us all is me. And I will have to be sent away, for the good of the Del Benes. Soon, I'll be gone from your life, Margherita. Will that make you sad?"

"You can act if you like; I won't. Yes, it will make me very sad."

He moved toward me, face to face. Even if he was older, he wasn't much taller than me. I noticed a hint of fuzz on his lip, and a mole on his neck.

"Do you love me, Margherita?"

He asked it in a sweet, unforgettable voice, and I looked down.

"I think I do," I answered.

"I don't love you," he cackled. "You see how evil I am?"

I didn't answer. The crickets held their breath, waiting.

He took my hand.

"I don't love you, I don't love anybody," he said. "But I thank you for bringing me here. You're like me in some ways. You invent names for things, you like to walk on the grass, you're afraid of people who are always right. We could have become friends. But I am in much greater danger than you are. My heart beats even fainter than yours."

"Angelo," I said, "don't go away. If there's something wrong, tell me about it, I'll help you."

He looked up at the sky.

"It's late, Margherita," he said. "And the stars are hiding. I've been happy once or twice. But I can't forget what I've seen. The fairytale has gone all wrong: the killers, Margherita, have become masters of the earth. There's no more room for us."

"I'm tired of this serious talk. Let's have some fun. I feel like climbing a tree. You want to try?"

"No. And how would you ever get up a tree, fat girl?" he said, giving me a kiss on one cheek and then bounding away like a hare.

"So long, beautiful dark angel, you shit!" I yelled after him.

Damned playactor, I thought as I headed home. I touched the cheek he had kissed, to see if it had turned to gold, or whether he had sucked my blood. I felt like crying.

Being in love, as both Plato and David Bowie have pointed out, is horrible.

I was home. In the yard in front of my house, a yellow light was gleaming. It wasn't the moon.

It was the flashing light of a police car.

I ran till my heart felt like it would burst. My mother threw open her arms to hold me.

"It was a hit-and-run accident. A motorcycle hit Grandpa, right here at the intersection. Don't worry, he has a few bad fractures, but he'll be okay."

I started crying. Then I flared up like a match.

"It was them!" I cried.

"You're crazy! Who are you talking about?" cried my dad.

"The Del Benes!" I yelled back, even louder. "They knew that Grandpa was spying on them and that he had discovered something."

"I forbid you to say such things about the Del Benes," he said. "They helped us again, this time. Frido even arranged for Grandpa to be admitted to a nursing home where he's a part owner. They are friends of ours!"

"They're all hypocrites," I yelled back. "But we're not going to take it anymore!"

I ran to the gate, pointing an accusatory finger at the black monster of a house.

"It was you, I know it was you!" I yelled. "Angelo told me it was you, and now I know who you are!"

Suddenly the gate swung open and out leapt Bozzo. He snarled and lunged at me. But Sleepy leapt heroically to protect me. I saw Bozzo's massive frame envelop the tiny body of my dog. My heart did a flip-flop, and I fainted.

I came to my senses in my bed. Mamma and my dad were looking down at me in concern. Heraclitus was holding Sleepy in his arms.

"Is that Sleepy's ghost?"

"No," Heraclitus explained in considerable excitement.

"When Bozzo went for him, Super-Sleepy dodged out of the way just in time, and then from behind he clamped his jaws onto Bozzo's balls. He held on until the monster-dog collapsed. Bozzo'll be barking like a Chihuahua from now on."

We all burst into laughter, including Sleepy.

"Do you still believe all those bad things you were saying?" asked Mamma as she stroked my hair.

"Mamma, why did they let their dog attack me?"

"You were yelling so loud that the dog couldn't hear the command to stop. They beat Bozzo silly afterwards. Do you think that they did it intentionally?"

"I think that . . . "

I rolled my eyes up and looked straight into the ceiling. What I saw there helped me decide what to do next.

"I think that . . . I've been unfair. And I don't want them to hurt their tankweiler, he's just a guard dog, it's in his chromosomes."

Dad and Mamma lit up like a pair of neon signs.

"The day after tomorrow, we're going to their house for dinner. You'll come too, won't you?"

"Certainly," I replied. "I'm curious to see their palace."

They turned out my light and left my room.

Soon I'll explain.

14. OLD PIETRO

The knight-errant Sir von Opferderlingstein rode out one day toward the forest of Wartburg.

The young and rebellious knight-errant, Sir von Opfwerdenlingen, rode out one day and, by a strange tree that had grown around an iron cross, he met a young maiden of incomparable beauty, whose name was Margherita.

The knight-errant, Sir von Opfendraklinden, was a vampire, but only a select few knew his horrible secret.

The knight-errant, Sir von Opferdelringhof rode out on his horse Sleepy early one morning, heading for the forest of Wartburg with the secret mission of slaying the emperor.

In the red forest of Wartburg there lived a beautiful maiden named Margherita Süssleben.

One day, as the knight errant, Sir von Opferwelingen, was riding on horseback through the forest, he met a young maiden weeping beside the smoking ruins of her home. Her hair was the color of dust . . .

The old Margherita Dolce Vita, because I am in fact aging, stayed in bed for only two days, but during that time she managed to write forty-seven first lines of novels, and then threw away all forty-seven. Dr. Heartthrob made a house call to check up on her, and said that her heart was still a little *ta-tunf-tatà*, but that if she kept taking her medicines, the nice little operation could be postponed for a while.

As you can certainly guess, oh daughter of mine, your Mamma was successfully operated upon, and now her heart is tired, but it pumps away reasonably well, like an old bicycle that has been faithfully maintained.

The day I went back to school was cloudy, and springtime had once again gone into hiding.

On the drive to school, I saw Labella go by. She was being driven to her high school in the dark blue limousine. She didn't even wave. I saw the usual streets, the usual stoplights, the usual apartment buildings under construction. Our neighborhood and the big city were about to meet in a tight, reinforced concrete embrace.

As I walked down the steps of the school bus, I realized something I had never noticed before: the school was cube-shaped. It was made out of old bricks and not Vetemprax, but it was still a cube. I took my usual seat, but there was a new development.

"Margherita, don't sit there," said my teacher. "Go sit next to Garzoni."

"Why?" I asked.

"Because you and Baccarini talk too much when you sit together."

I wasn't happy about the change. Piermaria Garzoni, along with the evil Gasparrone, the little Fascist Marra, and the bootlicker Venturini, constitute the royal flush of monsters in our class. Piermaria is the wealthy scion of Piergiuseppe Garzoni, the most ruthless and criminal builder and developer in our neighborhood. Playing shrewdly on the meaning of the term, "outskirts of town," he built *Aux Pears*, a "planned community" that is nothing more or less than a dozen horrible giant apartment towers, monstrosities that blight the landscape for miles around. Their name refers to "pears" because they are broad at the base and narrow at the top, an unsightly yellowish hue, and gloopy like overripe fruit (mainly because the plumbing is leaky and there are frequent floods). Obviously, the Garzoni development company skimped on materials. The towers are only a few years old, and already the walls are cracking and plaster is crumbling, accumulating at the base in a grim pear crumble. Clearly, the Garzoni family has some pear DNA in their chromosomes, because Piermaria is pear-shaped: a broad, fat ass, a stunted thorax, and atop his small head, a tufty stalk of hair that he slicks back, trendily.

The heir to the construction empire bared a smiling mouthful of teeth at me. I think he likes me. Lucky, lucky me. He was dressed in red and, looking closely, more than a pear, he resembled an enema bulb.

A nice start to a lovely day, I sighed to myself as I opened my backpack. The lesson was about Homer, but midst the clash of eternal battles, I was vanquished by a wine-dark wave of boredom, and I dozed until the bell rang.

When I awoke, there was a great hustle and bustle. La Baciolini was wearing a spectacular miniskirt, and Zagara must have dropped a hundred and sixteen pencils so that he could peep at her legs under the bench. The clatter of dropping pencils was so annoying that we finally begged her to take a picture of her panties and just give it to him so that he'd quiet down. La Baciolini giggled and told me that a black Cube had popped up near her house too. A very prosperous and likable family had moved in. The new neighbor girl had told her about a place that was having a sale on skirts. This miniskirt was a bargain at just 20 Euros. Cute, isn't it? And the neighbor had recommended a new hairdresser for her, too.

After break, the hall monitor came in and told us that the literature teacher, the one I liked best, wouldn't be coming today. A moped had clipped her father and he was in the hospital.

So school let out an hour early. At the exit, my math teacher, the terrifying Manson, stopped me. This time, though, she was as sweet as sugar. She said, "Margherita, your aunt came to see me."

"My aunt?"

"Yes indeed. What a nice lady! So refined . . . She came in for your parent-teacher conference, because your mother couldn't make it. She's not a bit like your mother, I mean, there's no physical resemblance. She wanted to know all about how you're doing, your strong points and where you're struggling. And she agreed completely when I said that you're a little too rebellious and strong-willed, and that you talk too much with Baccarini. She even gave me a perfume sample. A very refined woman."

"She certainly is," I said.

The Del Benes are behind this one, I thought. I boarded the school bus with the other kids, but I got off two stops early. I walked down to the river, to the fields that Pietro works. He is the last farmer in our neighborhood, and he lives in a shack by his fields. I know him because he sometimes sets up a farm stand along the road. He sells tomatoes and apricots and, if you order ahead, free-range chickens. When Heraclitus was a kid, he thought it meant that the chickens had been shot by marksmen on a firing range.

I walked toward the little farm, a miraculous cornucopia of abundance just three hundred yards from the main ring road. Pietro was working in his vineyard, which looked like rows and rows of magic broom handles planted in the soil. He was checking the grape buds, at least I think that's what they're called. All around him was a barnyard minuet of clucking hens. He gave me a big country smile.

"Signorina Margherita," he said. "What a pleasure! Did you come for the apricots? It's early yet."

"No, no," I said. "I had an hour free and I wanted to take a walk. How's work, Pietro?"

Pietro folded his arms across his chest and scratched the stubble on his chin. He is skinny, like Grandpa, but he looks as if he were whittled out of wood, with all the grain and even the knots.

"Not too pretty good. Yesterday a pair of fellows came down here and told me I had to get out."

"Why?"

"Well, they want to buy my land and build on it, though what they want to build they wouldn't say."

"What did you say to them?"

"I'm not sure I can tell you, *signorina*."

"Please. I've heard it all."

"I told them that they could stick their buildings up their ass."

"Well done."

"But last night, they stole my she-goats. I only had two, but I liked them. Who would want a couple of old nanny-goats? Not enough goat hair to knit a scarf."

"Well, Signore Pietro," I said. "If anything unusual happens, please give me a call!"

I realized that I was talking like a detective in an American movie.

"Unusual, like what?"

"Like, if they steal something, like your grapes. Or if the hens cluck . . . or caw . . . or cackle . . . or whatever you call the sounds chickens make, in the night. Or if your rabbits become impotent. Or if—"

"Signorina, what are you talking about?

"Pietro, what I am trying to say is: be on the lookout. Somebody wants to get their hands on your farm, and they aren't playing nice."

"I know, I know," Pietro said. "No one has ever played nice with me in my life. I'm used to it, you'd better believe it."

He picked up an old billhook and took a savage swipe at a gnarled vine.

"Are you taking it out on the grapevines, Pietro?"

"No, *signorina*. There are things that seem bad, and they are actually good. You can cut a branch to make a tree stronger, or else to make it weaken and die. There's a kind of rain that's good for the crops, and another kind that'll make them rot and die. You see that dust on the fig tree?"

"I see it."

"If that was dust from digging soil, it would be good. But that's from the factories around here. We call it dust, but it's lots of things mixed together: sand, pollen, smog, tiny germs, steam, poison, and who knows what all else. Do you know the story of the Dust Girl?"

"Yes, I know about her."

He leaned over close to me and spoke in a low voice, as if the hens might be eavesdropping.

"Well, I've seen her. Last year, when the bulldozers came to excavate the new interchange, and they knocked down the poplars. She was there, and she was watching. And when she gave them a certain look, the bulldozers would break down, and work would stop for half a day."

"Come on, don't try to frighten me . . . "

"You didn't grow up with a fireplace, did you?" asked Pietro, handing me a glass of wine that had appeared out of thin air.

"No, I . . . no, I don't think so."

"You didn't grow up with a fireplace, or a kerosene lantern, or a well with a bucket, did you? Well, you need to know that certain stories change, depending on where you hear them. If your grandfather tells you a fairytale, in a low voice, sitting around a fire burning in your fireplace, then, when your grandfather says, 'and then the devil burst into the room,' well, you feel like you can see the devil dancing, on the burning logs and sparks. And when you go to bed by candlelight, the story comes under the sheets with you. But especially, when you have to go to the well at night, by yourself, to crank up a bucketful of water, well that's when any story becomes scary."

"Would you tell me one?"

"A fireplace story, a candle story, or a well story?"

"A fireplace story."

"All right then, a sort of scary story. Once upon a time, there were two farmers. One was good-hearted and handsome, sort of like me, and the other one was wicked and lazy, and was named Berto. Berto was overbearing, he wasn't satisfied with his own land, and he wanted Pietro's land. Since Berto was wealthy, he had three cows and I don't know how many hogs and a slew of hens and a battery full of rabbits and geese as tall as a cavalry soldier . . . "

"So, he was rich . . . "

"That's right. So he wanted to buy Pietro's watermelon field. But these weren't just watermelons. They were wonders of nature, treasure chests, when you broke one open, it would crack like a rifle shot, and inside they were red, but redder than any blood on earth. Pietro loved his watermelons, he took care of them, he would coddle them, give them baths, and shine them till they gleamed, especially one watermelon in particular that he kept hidden beneath a hedge."

"Why?"

"I'll tell you afterward. So, Berto came to him and said, 'sell me your field,' just like one of those gentlemen yesterday. And Pietro said to him, 'no, I won't sell you the land,' just like I answered them. 'Because the watermelons are happy with the way I take care of them.' 'You old idiot,' Berto said, 'watermelons can't talk.'

"'Watermelons talk to one another, they are good friends, and they even have a king,' Pietro said. And Berto walked off, grimly, muttering dark threats. That night, Pietro woke with a start and heard a noise as if they were bombing his field. He went running, running, his heart in his throat, and the field was a bloodbath, all his watermelons had been dismembered, hacked and shot, the whole field was full of watermelon blood and juice, as if a thousand soldiers had been slaughtered in that field."

"How terrible."

"Terrible, indeed. So Pietro went to Berto and shouted at him, 'You damned murderer!' Berto laughed in his face. He sneered, 'Go on, tell your friends the watermelons to take revenge for their dead, you idiot.' And he laughed and laughed. That night, as soon as Berto went to bed, he heard the earth shake and the sound of thunderous, ponderous footsteps. He stepped out into the courtyard, and what did he see, in the pale moonlight? He saw the king of the watermelons, looming over him, as tall and stout as three strong men, advancing toward him, walking on its leaves, and a second later the watermelon lunged at him and . . . "

"And then what happened?"

"What happened, my sweet girl, is that the next morning, there wasn't a trace of Berto anywhere. They sent out parties to search for him everywhere, until nightfall. Someone swore that they heard his voice, pleading, 'help me, get me out of here!' But they never saw him again. Only Pietro knew that under a bush in his field there was an enormous watermelon, and it looked a little fatter than it had the day before. So be careful, young miss: there's always another mouth that's bigger and greedier than yours!"

"Br-r-r-r, that was scary . . . I won't be eating watermelon anytime soon."

"Aw, it's only an old fireplace story. Now, you'll have to excuse me, but I need to go see how Valencia is doing."

"Valencia? Is that your cow?"

"No, it's the finals match of the champion's cup in soccer: Valencia is playing Marseilles. Spain is challenging France, olé! Don't you follow soccer?"

No, I wanted to answer, but soccer sure follows me.

"Please, go watch your game, and I'm sorry if I've made you miss any of it," I said. "Enjoy the game."

He waved his hand and vanished into his little shack. I noticed that on top of the corrugated tin roof, there was a satellite dish almost the size of the one on the Cube.

For a moment I had a vision of the whole Valencia soccer team lined up in the stable, and a line of attractive soubrettes who were coming in to do the milking, but those images were a little too daring even for my young imagination, and I shut them out of my mind.

I got home, and there was a semi-trailer parked in front of the industrial shed. They had just unloaded a number of crates. My dad and Fedele were talking intently.

"What's in those?" I asked.

"Tools," my dad replied, with a hint of annoyance in his voice.

I looked at him closely. This was not my usual, exemplary father.

"Dad, what have you done to your head?"

"Nothing," he replied.

Nothing? Where his central bald spot used to be, there was a rakish little tuft. You could see it was artificial, because the hair stood straight up, as stiff as toothpicks, and the color was different from the rest of his hair, too.

"You're wearing a toupee!" I said.

"It's not a toupee. It's the Tricholuxuriase; it's kick-started the follicles, and now my hair is growing back."

"You look like you glued a slice of Sleepy onto the top of your head," I protested.

"Cut it out," my father said, angrily. "Don't be a pain in the neck, I am starting a new business to safeguard your future, and you bother me with silly questions! Get into the house."

He was definitely not the same.

Before going in, in any case, I checked to see whether Sleepy was missing anything, or if there was a patch sewn on. No, he was all there. So I walked into the house. And Giacinto was wearing a Dynamo sweatshirt.

"Ye Gods!" I said. "Tell me that it isn't true."

"Don't break my balls," he yelled. "A guy has a right to change his mind, doesn't he?"

I thought to myself: when a woman makes you change the way you live, you can laugh it off. But when a woman makes you change the soccer team you have always loved, the situation is serious.

"Giacinto," I said. "You do what you want; but I think that Labella is making a fool of you."

"You're right," he said, and he started to cry like a baby, his tears melting his pimple cream. A little stalactite of waxy cream began to form, a heartbreaking spectacle.

"I don't know what to do with myself, Margherita," he said between sobs. "I love her, I-love-her, *Iloveher* so mu-u-u-uch! Please, help me, teach me a trick, show me a book, give me a poem to win her heart."

"If you want to win Labella, I don't think books are the key," I explained to him, putting an arm around his shoulders. "I think that she is interested in other things. But, all the same, we could give it a try. Let's pick a snow-bound, romantic love story. Read *Anna Karenina*."

"Okay, let me write that down."

He wrote laboriously on a sheet of paper:

Anna Karenina, tennis player. Gorgeous.

I wanted to tell him that she wasn't a tennis player, she was a married woman who had an affair, but I knew that he'd never even try to buy that book. There he sat, 175 pounds of pheromones and flop-sweat, my poor big brother, exiled from Maraglistan.

"Tell me a story that I can use to charm her, to win her over," he begged.

"Okay, I'll tell you one. It's a legend."

"Like Maradona?"

"Older. Now then: Apollo and Hyacinth, who was a handsome young man whose name in ancient Greek was the same as yours in Italian, Giacinto, were close friends. They spent all their time together in the woods, engaging in sports and tossing a Frisbee back and forth. Back then, the Frisbee was a bronze, Olympic-quality disk that weighed twenty-two pounds. Since Apollo was an actual god, and was therefore very strong, one time he threw the Frisbee and Hyacinth was unable to catch it and the disk shattered his skull.

"Hyacinth lay dying on the earth, and he said, 'Apollo, my friend, you're a god, do something to help me.'

"'Okay,' Apollo answered.

"'You won't let me die?'

"'No, you'll die all right, but you'll then become a beautiful flower.'

"You understand now?"

"I need to ask Labella to play Frisbee with me?" asked Giacinto.

"No. You need to tell her this story and then say: 'Labella, if you and I become a couple, I don't want you to slay me with your divine beauty. I don't want to become a beautiful flower in your garden. Let me live, Labella, give me the life-giving power of your love.'"

"Well, I'll give it a shot," Giacinto said, slouching away uncertainly.

Poor Giacinto, he was really in a daze. However, maybe this unhappy love will make a real man of him. For that matter, maybe, if I keep thinking about Angelo, I, too, will become a real man.

And young Heraclitus?

He had aged too. He seemed to have forgotten his math

teacher. He had locked himself in his room, with that damned video game, gobbling down coconut snacks. He walked toward me, in a keyboard psychosis, his fingers continuing to tap in midair. He looked at me as if I were a strange creature, since I belonged to the animal kingdom, not the digital kingdom. Then he said, "I did it, but now I'm sad."

"What do you mean?"

"I finished Zelinda Four. I beat the ultimate boss, Mazuka-hokarakondorzo-kamizimashu. It was easy, really. You had to have the Rainbow Sword, reinforced with the four Stones of the Cosmos, and then you just needed to stab him seven times under the left gill, and then leap onto his tail to avoid the Fatal Breath, reinforce yourself with the Elixir of the Unicorn, and then once he's lost his wings, all you need to do is finish him off with a beam of Astral Light right in the mouth."

"So why are you sad?"

"Now what am I going to do all day? I hope that the Del Benes will give me Zelinda Five pretty soon."

I looked at him the way you would look at a flea.

"Erminio, I can't believe you are saying this to me. You, the scientific genius, the Pythagoras of the hinterland, the Galileo of the outlying quarters, the monstrous little brother that I used to respect, you who once gave me sage advice and lessons in astropataphysics, now you are nothing more than a pitiful little pixel junkie! You know what I say to you? If your math teacher could see you now, she'd kill herself, just like the Blue Fairy in Pinocchio."

"No!" he screamed.

"Yes!" I replied, and I knew that I had stabbed him with the Sword of Shame, and now I needed to finish him off with a beam of the Light of Extortion.

"Yes, you damned ingrate, one morning you'll go to school and in place of her desk, you'll find a sarcophagus with a marble statue of your math teacher and the legend:

I TAUGHT A CRETIN."

"No-o-o-o-o-o-o-o," screamed Heraclitus. "You can't say this to me, you shit! You're just saying this because you're jealous of Labella and the Del Benes."

"Heraclitus," I said calmly, "since you're so good at figuring out the tricks in video games, why don't you take a look at what's on the ceiling."

He looked at me, then he looked straight up and turned pale. Just then, Mamma came into the room. It was weird to see her. She smelled like Lenora, and she had the same hairstyle. She had even adopted the same little grimace. But worst of all, her skin was pulled tight. I know that she goes for Botox treatments. It's an operation of cosmetic sadism: they tie you to a chair, they give you injections in the face, and a horrible bacillus eats all your wrinkles and blemishes.

"Go get cleaned up, Margherita," Mamma said, with a Lenoric intonation. "You're filthy; where have you been?"

"I went to see Pietro, the farmer."

"I *will* not have you going to certain places!" she cried.

I felt like I was about to burst into tears. She understood, and she hugged me tight. I can sense that deep within her there is a battle raging between good and evil, between *Fais-moi du mal* perfume and bouillon cubes, between a meatloaf and a frozen TV dinner, between Mary Lou and Vanessa.

"I'm sorry," she said, dropping into a chair, as if she were suffering from vertigo. "I don't know what's happening anymore, there are too many new things happening all at once. Fausto refuses to fix my washing machine and he's filling the shed with who knows what. Giacinto is madly in love with that girl. Grandpa is locked up in that nursing home. All I can do is run my household. Without even the blessed happiness of a green stamp. I have to be . . . a good housewife, a good mother, a lady, you understand?"

"You're just you, Mamma."

"But our neighbors are watching, decorum is important, and so is your hairstyle." Now her eyes were wild and staring. "Because, as Mary Lou says in episode one hundred twelve: 'we are what we appear to be.'"

"But, as Robin says three episodes later: 'we don't always appear to be what we think we appear to be.'"

"Oh, Margherita," she said. "Why are you so intelligent?"

She said it with resignation, as if she had always dreamed of having an idiot daughter. I sat there, baffled.

"Mamma," I said to her. "Do you have a sister?"

"No."

"Then who is the aunt who attended the parent-teacher conference to find out about my performance at school?"

"I don't know anything about it," said Mamma.

She seemed sincere to me.

And we got ready for the second fatal dinner.

D uring the whole of a dull, dark, and soundless day,
when the clouds hung oppressively low in the heavens,
I had been walking through a singularly dreary tract of
country; and at length found myself, as the shades of the
evening drew on, within view of the melancholy House of Del
Bene. I know not how it was—but, with the first glimpse of the
building, a sense of insufferable gloom pervaded my spirit.

"What are you thinking about?" Mamma asked me, as I
straightened my fusilli-hair and we waited for the gate of the
Cube to open.

"A short story," I said.

"What short story?" my dad asked, suspiciously.

"Donald Duck and the Phantom of the River," I answered.
Forgive me, Edgar Allan.

There we were, all five of us in a line, waiting to be ushered
into the kingdom of the Del Benes.

My dad with his new turbohair and a three-piece pin-
striped suit that only a Mafia boss would wear.

Mamma in a brand-new soap opera suit, with a big greenbean-green brooch, holding a cake wrapped in Saran Wrap.

Giacinto wearing designer jeans, and one ear swollen with
a zirconium earring.

Heraclitus dressed like a Boy Scout about to be received
for a papal audience.

I was wearing the black outfit that everybody says makes me look two pounds lighter (so I really need to wear eight of them, one over the other).

Sleepy, who had not been invited to the party, watched us sadly from behind the hedge.

The gate swung open.

Bozzo, his eyes smoldering like coals, his testicles bandaged, looked at us as if we were five pork chops, but did not move.

The right side of the Cube opened silently.

At the door, Fedele Heitzmeesh, dressed in a white jacket and white Mickey Mouse gloves, gestured for us to step inside.

Here it was, the kingdom of the Del Benes.

A huge room, with useless-purple carpeting and a great big table made out of the usual black glass, already set for dinner.

The halogen lights cast a diffuse, chilly light, like an intensive care ward.

There wasn't a sofa or an easy chair.

Two huge Chinese vases, taller than me, and a table covered with Neolithic balls.

On the wall, just one painting: enormous and round, with an eagle holding a little animal in its claws, and an inscription.

The table was long and oval-shaped, as if for a political summit meeting.

And they were waiting for us.

Frido was wearing a navy blue blazer and had new hair, dyed a reddish hue, reminiscent of an orangutan's armpit.

Lenora was alluring, with her black suit, a moderate side vent or slit, and smoke-grey stockings.

Labella wore a skin-tight tracksuit, so close-fitting that even my dad turned to stare.

Angelo wasn't there.

At each seat, there was a place card with a name: Fausto, Emma, Labella, Margherita, and so on.

Frido didn't even come toward us; he just gestured, almost ordering us to take a seat.

That is what we did.

He sat down last, at the head of the table, so that behind him was the round painting with the eagle, just like on American television.

I squinted to see better, and I saw these words were written:

QUIS FUIT OPTIMUS PRIMUS QUI PROTULIT ENSES?

Now I know what those words mean; then, they meant nothing to me.

Fedele Heitzmeesh silently filled the little wine glasses with an aperitif. For me and Heraclitus, a pallid orangeade.

There was a bulletproof silence. I could hear every sound in the room.

The rumbling of Heraclitus's famished tummy.

Giacinto's love-crazed respiration.

The musical rattle of Labella's bracelets.

Mamma's self-conscious tapping as she tormented her fork.

The drone of the biohygienicized air.

Then Frido raised his glass and said, "A toast to this evening, when important decisions will be made."

Fedele Heitzmeesh brought in the antipasto.

A tiny bandage of salmon with a tiny turd of greenish sauce, laid atop a triangle of thin-sliced bread, with a base of four centimeters and a height of four centimeters, for a total area of eight square centimeters, and an olive perched on top.

*

The appetizer was gobbled down in seconds. The silence—in contrast to the food—grew heavy.

Then the pasta dish arrived: three ravioli each, with a black sauce, perhaps a walnut sauce, or perhaps just some of Frido's hair dye.

It should have been possible to devour them in just a few seconds. But between the first and second raviolo, Frido began to speak: "I have asked you here tonight to update you on our situation. In our neighborhood, there are lots of things that aren't going as well as we might like, but we are working to change those things, and it is a pleasure to have your support."

What is this? I wondered, and I looked over at my family. They all sat in rapt silence; only Heraclitus was busy filching Giacinto's third raviolo.

"We have gotten rid of the squeegee men at the intersections and the Gypsy camp, with all its thieves and muggers," Frido went on in a firm voice. "We have cleared the meadow, and set up adequate security systems. But this outlying area is still at risk. First of all, there is that farmer, Pietro, with his unsanitary shack, certainly in violation of all zoning regulations; he also has a stable that is probably filled with disease-carrying cows. And then there are those ugly ruins in the woods. I think that something much nicer could be built there. Right, Fausto?"

My dad nodded, his raviolo halfway to his mouth.

"And then, last of all, there are two families that have refused to sign our petition against petty crime in the neighborhood. One of the families, well, it's not hard to understand, they are Albanians, and claim to work as bricklayers. I sent the police to check on their residence permits. The other family is named Zagara; the father is from southern Italy. Now

I don't have anything against southerners, but all you need to do is walk by their house and you'll see what kind of people they are. Laundry hanging all over the place, garbage stacked up, even little plaster gnomes in the yard. I think that we need to help them to understand about good manners."

"Zagara is a classmate of mine, and he's a good kid," I said.

"One example of good manners is not to interrupt your host when he is speaking," said Frido.

You're taking off your mask, I thought. Now Dad will say something.

But everyone remained silent.

"But about good manners," Frido smiled, "and especially about the moral leadership that we are expected to provide as leading families in the neighborhood, Lenora will talk to you later. For now, let me just say that Fausto and I have gone into business together."

"Oh, how lovely," said Mamma, laying a hand on my dad's arm. "You didn't say anything, dear."

"I was waiting for the right time," Dad said, all puffed up with conceit.

"Yes, yes," Frido went on. "The shed is going to be the office and warehouse for an import-export company. Just for now, we're going to keep details confidential. The merchandise is quite unusual, and might well be attractive to industrial spies. So, please, let's not talk about it to outsiders."

"Is it video games?" asked Heraclitus in a hopeful tone of voice.

"It's something that is going to make your father a wealthy man," said Frido. "And it strikes me that that is the first rule of business."

"Honest business, of course," I added.

"Well certainly," said Mamma, smiling at my dad.

"Honest is an old-fashioned word," said Frido. "Let's just say, in compliance with the laws of the market."

"Speaking of old-fashioned, how is Grandpa?" asked Lenora. And she looked a little cross-eyed in my direction; it scared me.

"Oh, he's all right," answered my dad, testily.

"We'll talk about that after the meal," said Frido. "Here's the entrée."

Creamed cod, the promise had been kept. But with just one cod to share among eight people. There were also tiny potatoes, or maybe they were yellow peas.

"Are you still hungry, little boy?" asked Lenora, as she noticed that Heraclitus was stealing po-pea-toes from Giacinto, who in the meantime was nourishing himself with Visions of Labella.

"I think that after dinner there will be a surprise for Erminio," said Labella.

"I've had quite enough," said Heraclitus, very properly.

You little hypocrite. Even you have turned against me.

"In just a minute, it will be time for dessert," said Lenora. "But first I need to say something that for some of you will be something of a bitter pill."

She stood up as if she were delivering a lecture, and her voice changed, as if it had been deformed by an evil microphone.

"I have to say that I am just a little disappointed. I have lavished attention on you, advice and tips on how to improve yourselves, but I see that much of my advice has not been followed. You, Fausto, continue to let that horrible little dog run free, and my beloved Bozzo has already suffered one unfortunate injury. I would like to repeat my suggestion that you put that dog on a chain, otherwise I will be forced to summon the dog catcher."

"But Lenora . . . " Mamma exclaimed.

"Hush, please, say no more," Lenora said. "You, too, Emma, often behave less like a star of 'Eternal Love' than one might hope, and much more like a silly and ordinary housewife. I have told you a thousand times not to do your hair that way, I have told you that you should never wear brooches and necklaces with a suit of that kind. And you will kindly remember in future that you don't show up carrying dessert when you are a guest at a dinner party of this quality; please! We are not in Sicily!"

"I won't let it happen again," Mamma murmured, abashed.

"I certainly hope not. I would suggest you go back and reread with some care the *Manual of the Little Ambassador* that I lent you. And let me also ask you to pay the final bill for the Bio-Ionized Air system; kindly recall that I personally asked them to make sure that the system was installed on a rush basis. I hope that I won't be caused any embarrassment. And I must—I repeat I must—ask you to take better care of your yard; it's overgrown with weeds and flowers, and the bugs and the dust blow over to our house. And, as you know, *I hate dust*. Last of all, I don't like you to do your grocery shopping in that cooperative supermarket, which offers green stamps and probably also finances Communist dictatorships. There is a much more reliable and responsible supermarket a mile or so from here."

"Mamma," I whispered, "do you hear what she is saying?"

Mamma seemed petrified, frozen in the basilisk glare of Medusa Lenora. And the Gorgon swiveled her baleful eyes in my direction.

"As for you, Margherita, things are just not right with you. I went in to have a conversation with your teachers."

"Who gave you right to do that?" I practically screamed.

"I asked your father's permission. Among my responsibilities is to monitor the morals of my daughter's friends."

"Then you'd better keep an eye out for Pataffas . . . "

"What?"

"Oh, nothing, nothing," I said. I may be mean, but I'm not a tattletale. Labella had turned red as a tomato.

"Now then, Margherita, you are still sitting next to a girl who is just . . . too lively, a certain Baccarini. It was me who asked them to separate the two of you. Moreover, they told me that you spend half your time reading books that aren't even in the curriculum. As a result, you waste your time, and you're a bit weak in other subjects, like math . . . "

"That's my business," I said.

"Silence," hissed the harpy. "And for the last time, I forbid you to walk through these wild, dangerous fields with my son, Angelo, taking him who knows where to do who knows what."

I was about to say something to her that would have made a whole team of porn stars blush, but Fedele Heitzmeesh chose that moment to bring in dessert.

A slice of a slice of cake. I didn't even touch it. Heraclitus swooped down like a swift little falcon and gobbled it up.

"Margherita," Mamma said, uncomfortably, "I can certainly understand that you might be a little irritated with Lenora's observations, but she cares about you, and that's why she's taking an interest in you."

"She should care a little more about her own son," I couldn't help saying.

"Margherita," my dad said. "Shut your mouth. How dare you?"

"Shut my mouth? The hell with that!" I exclaimed, banging my fork on the table. "Where's Angelo? Why do you keep him hidden away? Are you ashamed of him? Do you want to get rid of him? All right, now it's time for me to deliver a little sermon to you all. You, too, are a bit weak in certain subjects."

"Labella, go to your room," Lenora said. "I don't you to be subjected to this sort of talk."

Labella got up from the table and stuck her tongue out at me as she left. Giacinto followed her like a puppy.

A mantle of silence fell on vases, balls, and wall-to-wall carpeting.

Then Frido unsheathed the most precooked smile he possessed. "Calm down, everyone," he said. "This is just a friendly dinner, let's not forget. If you think that we are meddling in your lives, please, just say so. But don't forget, we're doing it out of affection, the same feelings that we have for our unfortunate son."

"Out of affection," Lenora reiterated.

"They're doing it out of affection," said Mamma.

"Crap," I muttered under my breath. "Mamma, it's not out of affection. There's something else going on here. They don't mean a thing they say."

"Erminio," Frido said, who might have overheard. "Do you think we're insincere?"

Heraclitus don't betray me, at least not you.

"I just think that Margherita is a little upset," he said. "In fact, I think that she has a major crush on your son."

A burst of fake laughter broke the tension.

"Young, but wise," said Frido.

"Young, but wise, and with ulterior motives!" exclaimed Heraclitus with a comic grimace. "Doctor Frido, tell me, are you familiar with a video game called Zelinda and the Perfidious Laughing Dragon?"

"Of course I am," answered Frido. "We're expecting the first delivery this week. You will be my primary game tester."

"Excellent," said Heraclitus.

I was about to stab him with my fork under the table, the treasonous mini-bastard, when he intentionally dropped a utensil and, as he bent over, whispered in my ear: "There is no such game as Zelinda and the Laughing Dragon, I made it up just now."

Good old Heraclitus, now I know that I can count on you.

Labella and Giacinto came back into the dining room.

"Giacinto just told me the story of the most beautiful old myth," said Labella.

"Really? Why don't you tell us the story too?" said Lenora.

"Sure," said Giacinto. "There was a guy named Giacinto, more or less like me, but in ancient Greece, and he and Apollo were playing Frisbee. Apollo was a cool dude, and he smacked him upside the head, and the Frisbee—well, it was a bronze Frisbee—crushed Giacinto's skull. 'What the fuck were you thinking,' said Giacinto. So Apollo turned him into a flower."

There was a moment of silence.

"How unusual," said Lenora.

"Very poetic," said Mamma.

"I don't get it," said my dad.

"Well," said Frido, "I certainly don't want this unseemly tension to persist. Let's make peace. My dear, my impertinent young Margherita," and he raised his glass in my direction with a courtly and convivial gesture; "Angelo is not here, because he is receiving medical care. He is spending a few days in a quiet place. We hope that his nerves get better soon. But, please tell me, what did you and he talk about?"

You're not going to trick me, you sly fox.

"Books," I said.

"Anyway, our son should not be wandering around unsupervised," Frido said to his wife with a note of reproof. "Well, let's finish with up with two pieces of news. One is good news, and the other is so-so. Which do you want first?"

"There is one piece of good news and one piece of bad news in every episode of 'Eternal Love,'" said Mamma. "And normally they give the bad news at the end, right before the theme music."

"All right. First the good news: tomorrow Fausto and I are going to begin working seriously. We're going to carry out a first . . . inspection. Right, Fausto?"

"Well, actually, I didn't think it would begin this soon."

"You can't say no, Fausto," Frido said, staring at him. "Only you and I know what's in the shed."

"Well, all right," answered my father.

"And we'll take Giacinto with us. Will you come with us, Giacinto?"

"Yes, Giacinto, don't you want to go with them?" said Labella, and she laid her delicate little hand on his great big hand.

Giacinto slid from a coma to a heavenly smile and said, "I do . . ."

As if he were at the altar.

"What about the so-so piece of news?" asked Mamma.

"Well," said Frido, "today I had a conversation with Dr. Totalstud from the Santa Vispa nursing home. He said that your grandfather's fractures are very serious. It's impossible to operate. For now, he needs to remain under their care, in the hope that the fractures knit on their own."

"How long?" asked Mamma.

"There's no saying," said Frido. "But you should be prepared for the worst: he may never walk again."

"That's not a piece of so-so news," I said. "That's terrible news. Poor Grandpa!"

"At his age, he had no business walking around on his own," Frido said harshly.

"Just like Angelo, right? Or like me, since I have heart disease. No one should be allowed to go around unsupervised if you and your friends don't like it, right Doctor Frido?"

"That's right, Margherita. And please remember that one of my friends is your father."

"I'm honored that you should say so," my dad said.

"Dad, I'm ashamed of you," I said to him.

He came toward me, and as he did his toupee slid over one eye. He drew back and smacked me—hard—across the face. I didn't even try to dodge it. I couldn't believe that he would do it. Now I know that he could, and it hurts me worse than the smack across the face.

Though the smack across the face sure hurt like hell.

17. VISITING GRANDPA

Nothing more was said about the smack in the face; it was an isolated episode, as people say in these cases. But nobody spoke during breakfast.

Mamma had started non-smoking again, one nervous Virtual after another. Dad, as if old times had returned, pretended to repair a bicycle. But the bike fought back, and bit one of his hands with the handbrake cable. You can fool bipeds, but not velocipedes. Heraclitus claimed to be sick but I knew that, in the privacy of his room, he was scheming.

I went to school, and I immediately sent an anonymous note to Zagara:

Zagara, you are in danger. Someone who cares about you.

I felt like adding: *maybe the only one.*

I didn't know what else I could do. Then my math teacher asked me how my aunt was.

"Well, ma'am, I'm sorry to say that she was arrested yesterday," I answered. "The police found her prostituting herself on the ring road, with a purse full of cocaine, dildoes, and pornography."

"Really!" said my teacher. "She seemed so respectable, so . . . "

"So . . . normal, right? Never judge from appearances."

She walked away, shaking her head.

*

After school, I didn't feel like going home. I left a message on the home answering machine that I wouldn't be back till later. And I emptied my coin purse to take a taxi. I went to visit Grandpa in the nursing home.

The Santa Vispa private clinic and nursing home is at the top of a hill, and it is possible to enjoy—or suffer—a panoramic view of the entire city. The place reeks of lilies and chamber pots. At the entrance, a bust of a famous doctor enjoys pride of place, and a plaque informs all who pass that during his lifetime, that man behaved in an exemplary manner. Very much like the bust at the main entrance to my school.

Just once I would like to see a handsome marble bust with this inscription:

IN COMMEMORATION OF THAT SON-OF-A-BITCH LIAR AND CHEAT
WHO BLIGHTED THE CIVIC LIFE OF THIS TOWN
WITH HIS MANY MISDEEDS.
MAY HELL CONSUME HIS SOUL.
REMEMBER THIS FACE.
IT IS THE FACE OF A DOUBLE-DEALING SWINE.

I'd know who to dedicate it to. But let's get back to our story. The nursing home, as I have said, looks a lot like my school. In fact, it was full of octogenarian children. Grandpa was waiting for me in a wheelchair, his feet sunk in two enormous yellow duck-shaped slippers.

He was skinny and ashen-faced, and he smiled at me. It was clear that he was doing his best to seem cheerful. I did the same. As a result, before long, we both burst into tears.

But then he said, "Cheer up, girl, sooner or later I'll get out of here." And to show that he was in full vigor he uttered two or three oaths and obscenities that would have knocked a swarm of saints out of the sky, then he introduced me to the other guests, one by one.

There was Don Karloff, a former priest who ululated and cursed like a trooper all day long; it sounded like the sound track of a horror movie. Then there was Chantal, a berouged eighty-year-old who sang the same song over and over in a thin, reedy voice, perhaps it was "In My Gaze is the Elixir." In one corner, a little old lady bent over with arthritis like a wire sculptor's dummy was tatting away with invisible embroidery needles. Two elderly gents with jaundice sat playing a century-long game of checkers.

The table with the most lucid and diabolical old ladies, known jocularly as "the weird sisters," contemplated the surrounding landscape of senility with a superior air. The elegant Signora Fornara sat reading *VIP 2000*. The ponderous Berta, weighed down with jewelry and a swoopy turban on her head, sat snoring and farting on her throne of a chair perched on a little dais of water cushions. The head of the tribe, the almost century-old Callista, an Apache brave in a sky-blue dressing gown, was playing a hand of solitaire and muttering to herself.

She noticed me and said, "Good afternoon, commissioner, when are you going to take us to the beach?"

"We're looking into it, we're looking into it," I answered.

I sat down next to Grandpa and began telling him about the dinner at the Del Benes, but he fell asleep. He was snoring and whistling at the same time. I waited. A woman pushing a geriatric walker on wheels went by, walking and counting. I heard her say, "Eleven thousand three hundred and one, eleven thousand three hundred and two." A smiling black nurse picked up a little grandmother, as weightless as a newborn baby, and placed her gently in a high chair.

I tried to remember what this place was reminding me of.

Of course, my nursery school!

On the wall there were drawings with flowers and bees, and the sentence: "The sun is shining today." Even though it wasn't. It really did look like a nursery school full of little children, of lives rewound backwards. A return to mindless babbling, nursery rhymes, and sudden bursts of weeping, dribbling spoonfuls of pablum, endless chants of caca-caca-caca, unexpected gusts of enthusiasm and hopeless abysses of terror. And just like with children, they would play dead. If one day you happened to see a new face at the dining room table, it just meant that a place had opened up. All you had to do was check to see who was missing. And yet, how could you explain that clot of irrepressible life, those tantrums, the little welling desires, those fingernails gripping fiercely to the edge of the abyss? And the joy of the all-too-rare smiles, the anticipation of a visit, a slice of cake, a blackbird on the windowsill . . .

I remembered the way it was when I would go to visit my Aunt Venusta in the hospital. I would walk in fearfully, but when I left I was practically dancing. I would feel healthier, stronger. The fleeting joy of the survivor.

But there was more than just death in there. There was tenacious, ironic life. Moss on the smooth, hard rock.

"Stop thinking," said Grandpa, as he woke up.

He kicked his skinny little feet in the giant duck slippers, and I saw that the pockets of his dressing gown were full of candy. A baby-Grandpa, eighty-plus years old.

"Please, help me," he whispered. "That lady over there, Signora Pica, stole my dentures. See if you can get them back."

I singled out the thief. She was sitting in a corner, her bag filled with the booty from her petty thefts.

"Signora Pica," I asked patiently, "did you take my grandfather's dentures?"

"No," she protested. "It was the new patient, that Chinese

guy, the yellow man who plays checkers. He's a wicked man. He wants to marry me, but I told him I wouldn't go along with it."

She pointed at him, with one skinny claw. I rummaged through her purse. There were a few pieces of bread, a hand mirror, and three sets of dentures. I recognized Grandpa's dentures.

"Don't report me," Signora Pica whimpered.

"Not this time," said Grandpa. "But next time I'll tell the head nurse, or maybe I'll send ghosts to your room."

Signora Pica crossed herself. Grandpa reinserted his false teeth with a triumphant grimace.

"Did you bring me any detergent to flavor my soup?" he asked.

"The doctors say that you need to get over that obsession."

"Screw the doctors. In here, I'm like a guppy in a fishbowl. When I was at home, at least I was free to be an eccentric nut. Now, I can't even do that."

I turned my back to him and started crying, pretending I was looking out at the landscape.

"Margherita, cut it out," Grandpa said. "I'm not doing so badly in here. I grab the nurses' asses and I put the blame on the priest. I steal semolina from the food cart; my spoon's always at the ready in my pocket. Every time they take my blood pressure I fart to see if I can make the gauge jump. And then, Doña Lupinda comes to see me every night."

"Do you dance?"

"Certainly. I get out of bed and I dance."

"What about her husband?"

"We killed him, and we buried him in the Del Benes' yard, with all the others."

"Grandpa, what are you saying?"

"Nothing, nothing. But I can tell you're sad, Margherita Dolce Vita. Dad and Mamma have changed, haven't they?

And Giacinto. And I am afraid that all this will transform Heraclitus, too. Are you afraid that something bad is going to happen?"

"No, Grandpa, no. But I do see such strange things . . . "

"What about your blond sweetheart?"

"Well, we see each other every so often but, well, I didn't think love was so stressful, that's all."

If you meet an angel, you will have not peace, but a fever.

"Who wrote that?"

"An epileptic poet."

"I'm writing a book too, Grandpa. The adventures of the knight, Sir von Opfernlinden and the Dust Girl. It begins with a scene where he goes riding through the woods. I'm pretty well into it."

"You've written three lines, if I know you at all. But you look out for Dust Girl. She may be your sister and she may be your friend, but if you touch her, you'll never be the same. They stole her childhood, and she'll steal yours. You can't look everything in the eyes, Margherita."

"Is that why you look through your spyglass?"

Grandpa laughed and stretched in his wheelchair. He began to declaim as if he were on a stage.

"Oh, I saw her many years ago, that eldritch little girl. I followed the beams of her eyes through terrible storms. I was shipwrecked by love of a siren. I visited the most far flung, boundless oceans, but none of them was as vast as our meadow."

"Did you ever see the King of the Watermelons?"

"Oh yes, I saw him devour wicked men and copulate with the Queen of the Pumpkins. But I am joking, and you are still sad, Margherita."

"No, what on earth are you saying?"

"You can't lie to your captain," Grandpa said, as he stroked my hair. "Is this place making you sad? Are you afraid that the disease of old age might infect you? Poor Margherita, the real disease is outside, it's rotted hearts and souls. But let's stop talking like this: don't come to visit me again, I don't want to be a burden to anyone."

"Grandpa, don't talk nonsense."

"Oh, I'm never going to get out of here," he sighed, looking out of the window. "Tell me, are the poppies blooming in the meadow?"

"Yes, but it's still cold. It's not really spring yet."

"In here, it's always winter," Grandpa said. "You can fill the whole place with flowers, but it's still always winter. Nothing ever happens. Just the names and ages change. One dies, another one takes their place. You see that one over there, the one that arrived yesterday? The one with a little mousy face, with whiskers?"

"I see him, Grandpa, don't point."

"Oh, it doesn't matter, he's blind. He walks around banging into doors, and Signora Pica steals stewed apples from under his nose. They brought him in to take the place of Elvira, a lady who used to just sleep all the time. One night she went to bed, and then at midnight, she asked for a glass of water. The nurse brought her the water, and she died right then, the glass of water in her hand, pouring onto the bedclothes like a little statue in a fountain."

"Pardon me," whispered a tiny little voice behind me. I turned around and saw a tiny little old lady balanced at the edge of a chair.

"I'm not dead," said Elvira. "Tell you're grandfather that I'm alive. It was La Fragaglini who died; she used to eat at the same table as me, the one with the tremor."

"I'll tell him, please forgive him, maybe he was confused."

"What is that woman saying to you?" asked Grandpa, suspiciously.

"She says that she is Elvira," I explained. "And that she's alive, and that it was another lady who died."

"Then who told me Elvira was dead?" Grandpa exclaimed loudly. "What damned fool told me she was dead? Berta, it was you, wasn't it?"

"Me?" Berta bellowed in her resounding voice. "You dreamt it, you ass-grabbing idiot!"

This triggered a dispute that rolled from chair to chair. I tried to calm them down, but I couldn't even figure out what was happening. The temporarily living accused the dead of not being dead and generating a lot of useless mourning; indeed, of trying to get others to die in their place. Luckily, the meal cart rolled up, accompanied by a pacifying cloud of aromas.

They all gathered around the tables, spinning the wheels of their wheelchairs in their eagerness. "Oh boy, macaroni!" shouted one excited voice. And, "Oh hell, macaroni again!" cried another disappointed voice.

I wheeled Grandpa up to his place at the table, I tied his bib around his neck, and said, "Eat up, Grandpa."

Shooting me a wink, he pulled a can of talcum powder out of one pocket and sprinkled it over his pasta.

"No, Grandpa!" I said.

"I'm habituated, I'll survive this place too. I'm going to live long enough to see that damned Cube burn to the ground," he said.

"That's right, Grandpa, be strong, maybe the worst is over."

"No," he said with a sigh. "The worst is yet to come, Margherita. Don't try to call horror by different name. That's their job, let them do their worst."

"But you always told me to keep my hopes up," I whispered, holding his hand. Grandpa thought that one over for a minute, his sharp little chin resting between both hands.

"I believe that there will always be intelligence, a yearning for liberty, Eros, and dance halls," Grandpa said. "But the word hope, well, I'm not sure I'm ready to use it."

I felt a huge stereoscopically symmetrical tear, about to burst out of me.

"Give me one of your famous words of wisdom before I go, Grandpa."

"All right."

The Earth is right-wing, the Universe is left-wing.

"That gives me a lot of food for thought," I said. "I'll give your regards to Heraclitus."

"Don't bother. He knows everything that happens to me," said Grandpa, and as he said it, he wore the same cunning smile as my little brother.

I went back home, and saw that same huge semi-trailer, and standing around it were my dad, Fedele Heitzmeesh, Frido, and two questionable characters wearing sunglasses. Dad came toward me, and I instinctively covered my face with both hands.

"Don't be afraid of me," he said affably. "I'm sorry about the slap; I was just very tense yesterday. This new business is a good thing, but I must be a little rusty when it comes to doing real work, just like an old bicycle. I have to oil up my thinking a little."

"Of course," I said. "Your new, mysterious business."

"Would you like to know what's in the crates, Margherita?" Frido asked.

"Why not?" I said, in a challenging tone of voice. Frido thought it over for a moment. Then he nodded to Fedele Heitzmeesh.

"All right," he said. "Go on, open a crate."

Fedele Heitzmeesh opened one, and legs, arms, and hands came tumbling out.

"They are prosthetic limbs, artificial arms and legs for children," my dad explained. "Frido exports them to war-torn nations. And, just so you know, it's not for profit. Frido's company invests twenty percent of the revenues in charity, and it ships these limbs to countries in every corner of the earth."

I stood there, dazed, holding a plastic foot in one hand.

"Do you think that this is work I shouldn't be doing?" asked my dad.

"Your father," Frido explained, "will be in charge of the African territory, just for starters."

"Well, Dad," I said, "this is socially beneficial work. I'm proud of you."

"Then, will you promise to stop poking around the shed?" asked Frido.

"Okay," I said.

Could I have been wrong about them?

I had just become acquainted with Frido's new role as humanitarian, but I was still uneasy. I was watching my parents change, day by day; I hardly recognized them anymore. The same with Giacinto. Heraclitus was too young to help me, and Grandpa was being held captive far away. As for Sleepy, he was out on love safari all day, every day. After having met Bozzo, he was only interested in bitches twice his size. He would scale them bravely but in vain, and would come home disappointed and horny, only to take it out on poor Pontius.

Complaining was pointless; the time had come to fight. If you surrender at fourteen, you'll get used to surrendering for the rest of your life.

Only dead fish move with the current.

That's what Grandpa used to say. So I decided to stay cool and keep my eyes wide open.

First of all, while my dad was out watering the yard, I decided to make a little inspection of my parents' bedroom, in the eastern, paternal quadrant.

I know that was wrong, but war is hell. And nowadays, spying is called intelligence. So I rummaged intelligently through all his dresser drawers.

I found a clump of hair, his spare toupee, and a few bottles of hair dye, in mahogany, black, and noir sauvage. Most interestingly, under a layer of underpants, I found a pistol.

On the box was written: "Starter's pistol, shoots blanks only."

Sure, I thought, it's not a real gun, but Frido has already half won him over.

Then I inspected the western, maternal quadrant.

In the drawer of the night table, there was nothing interesting. But under the bedside rug there was an envelope of green stamps. I should have known.

In the bathroom, on the other hand, I found ten boxes of a pharmaceutical called CelluSlimmex.

An anti-cellulite treatment.

I looked at the sheet with warnings about side effects. You name it: sleepiness, depression, psoriasis, coma, hirsutism and hypertrichosis (unwanted hair growth, also known as human werewolf syndrome), and even Weissmuller's syndrome.

Basically, it could make you come down with practically everything, except for cellulite.

I went looking for Mamma and found her, as usual, in a trance before the plasma monster-screen. She was watching a show where a guy said that his girlfriend had been cheating on him, and his girlfriend retorted, "Sure, but you were always going to the swimming pool," and the studio audience burst into applause.

"Mamma," I asked her. "Who told you that you have cellulite?"

She turned and saw that I was holding a box of CelluSlimmex.

"Lenora told me that if I take that medicine for six months, I'll improve. I had never noticed, but I am full of unsightly bumps and dimples."

"Mamma, you're fifty years old, it's just normal."

"Oh, don't say that," she whimpered. "Look at Mary Lou.

She's been acting in 'Eternal Love' for twelve years and she looks just as young as in the first episode."

"Mamma, you have been watching those episodes for the past twenty years, but she probably shot them in two years. Right now, Mary Lou is probably a 220-pound American butterball stuffing herself with chunks of chocolate."

"Don't say such things," Mamma sniffled. "Why are you trying to destroy my dreams?"

"Okay, Mamma, okay," I said. "Cram yourself with vampire lotions and carnivorous botulins, but beware of the side effects. If you start to grow whiskers like Sleepy, let me know."

"We have to suffer, if we want to be beautiful," she declared bravely.

"Yeah, who told you that? Lenora, Mary Lou, or the Baroness von Masoch?"

"The Baroness who?"

"Never mind. Where's Giacinto?"

"He went with Labella and her friends to see the championship game."

"There's no soccer championship game today."

"No, it wasn't soccer, it was some other sport. Let me see . . . Oh yes, it was golf . . . "

"Are you sure of that?"

"Yes. It was a golf tournament, up in the hills."

I recalled a detail. A few months ago, when Giacinto was still a right-thinking soccer hooligan, he had said, "If you ever see me go bowling, or play polo, please, kill me."

He hadn't mentioned golf.

I had just one more chance to raise my spirits: Heraclitus.

But the next day, there was a math exam, and he was studying.

No, he wasn't studying, he was lifting weights.

He claims that Miss Stork likes muscular little boys.

I was at my wits' end, and I silently prayed: Little sister of mine, help me now.

Well, she heard my prayer.

I saw a cloud of dust outside the window. But it wasn't dust, it was exhaust fumes. I heard the noise of a moped, and there he was, downstairs, with a red bandanna around his neck and an extra helmet for me, and he yelled, "Come on, Margherita Dolce Vita, I'm on furlough from the insane asylum. I'll take you for a nice ride."

I was ready and downstairs in fifteen seconds. And we were off, my arms wrapped around his jacket, zooming down the romantic straightaways of the industrial hinterland. The wind tousled my hair and hoisted my skirt, and every so often a driver would look because, well, I may not be a top model but panties are panties, right? Angelo kept the throttle at full, but luckily the moped was a pathetic old wreck, and wouldn't go very fast.

"I missed you!" I yelled into his ear.

"I can't hear you!" he lied back.

We stopped at a spot on the elevated road where it ran close to a row of houses.

Angelo got off the moped, paying no attention to the cars that went zipping past, and leaned over the guardrail.

"Look at that," he said to me.

There was an old apartment building, with windows exactly on a line with the roadway. Just a few yards away, directly across from us, on the fourth floor, there was balcony with two old people. He sat reading the newspaper, and she was watering the geraniums. There was laundry hanging out to dry, a birdcage with a canary, and a cat standing guard. The gusts of wind from the passing cars tossed the legs of the pajama bottoms like a flag blowing bravely in a stiff breeze, and the wafting clouds of gasoline and smog had muted the song of the little bird. The vibrations from the passing trucks shook the windows and their dentures. But still they persisted, sitting peacefully in the sun, between the passing shadows of one semi-trailer and the next.

"Twenty years ago, this was countryside," I said. "But maybe someone should tell them that there have been some changes."

"Whenever I go by here, this sight just enchants me," Angelo said. "They're tough old birds, and they're not giving up. There's no toxic gas or intolerable noise that could drive them away. Sometimes I come by here at night, and I watch them eating dinner, facing one another across the table. Or else they play cards. The world goes racing past them, and they never change."

"Would you want to be like them?"

"I don't know," said Angelo. "Maybe they're just dazed, and they're waiting to die. Or else they have something inside them that we don't have."

"Now I'll show you something," I said,

"If it's your panties, I've already seen them."

"Cradle robber. You're two years older than me."

"But you're bigger than me!"

I chased after him, trying to hit him as we ran along the edge of the elevated road, with drivers honking as they passed and yelling insults at us out their windows. Then, both laughing, we got back onto the moped and drove off.

"Turn right here, take that little alley running up the hill," I said.

The moped climbed, the rear tire fishtailing along the gravel lane, until we reached a big clearing high above the main road. It was a little mountain of excavated dirt; not far away was a foul-smelling garbage dump. From there, we could see the whole city and even the Cube and my house, the sea of grass, and far away in the distance something that might be the silhouette of the mountains, lost in the lowering smog.

Behind us was a long cement embankment, with lots of cracks running down its face.

Life had reserved it a happy fate.

There was a spectacular expanse of graffiti painted across it, at least a hundred feet of colors.

Dragons, gnomes, black jazz musicians wailing on the sax, sirens and tropical birds, cocks, tits, exotic fruit, Cyclopes, cannabis leaves and calibans, a yellow submarine, and a number of phrases, including one in particular that stood out from all the rest, an enormous:

WE DON'T BELIEVE YOU ANYMORE.

That giant mural had been the work of many artists. Three of them had signed their names:

Vincent van Bongh, Canapone da Caserta, and Maya Kovsky.

"That's great," said Angelo. "Those guys know how to use their coloring cases, don't they?"

"Every time they do one, the authorities come and paint it over or sandblast it off, and each time that happens, they paint a new one, in a different place," I said.

"I know," Angelo sighed. "My dad always calls city hall, or else he pays a painting company himself to come and cover them up."

"Why does he care?"

"Well, he can't sell them," said Angelo.

Just then we noticed that, at the far end of the wall, somebody was painting. It was a tall, skinny young man, with slightly mascaraed eyes and a carrot-red beard. I ventured a wild guess.

"Are you Vincent van Bongh?"

"Yeah, baby," he said. "Why do you want to know?"

"We just adore your graffiti," I said, with the voice of a fan.

"I could not care less," he replied calmly. "We are just dilettantes. In the old days, they were good, really good."

"In the old days, when?"

"Millions of years ago," said Vincent, setting down his can of spray paint and looking into the distance, toward the far horizons of the past. "Have you ever seen prehistoric cave paintings? Mammoth hunts? That was real graffiti. You know why?"

"Not really," answered Angelo, amused.

"Who do you think did those paintings?"

"Well, cavemen, right?" I replied.

"Wrong," said Vincent. "A friend of mine who is a paleontologist has studied those paintings carefully. And he has determined that they were sketched with something very big and very very hard. Nothing that has anything to do with the tools that humans made back then."

"So?"

"So, he investigated further, using exceedingly sophisticated technical methods, and he finally found proof. Ivory dust and thick hairs in the grooves. The artist who did those paintings was not a human. It was a mammoth."

"No kidding," Angelo and I said in unison.

"Really," said Vincent. "It was a mammoth. He very skillfully and carefully used his giant head, and his tusks. Only a mammoth could describe the fear of the chase, the tragic drama of the hunt. He had lived those scenes in the first person, or first pachyderm. That's what art is: escaping everyday normality, which wants to eat you alive. I'm always on the run, and my art looks the way it does because I know it can be erased, devoured in an instant. And yet I know that one of these murals will survive, at least, or maybe many of them, and they will last for millions of years. I am a mammoth."

There was no time to answer him. Van Bongh descended the slope, leaping from rock to crag like a prehistoric chamois. We saw him run across the road and vanish.

After this little adventure, we roamed around for a while on the side streets, amidst babbling brooks and fields of alfalfa. On one straightaway, we sighted a swarm of gigantic yellow-jackets. They were an elderly cycling club, wearing yellow-and-black outfits and riding Ingrids. Their plump bottoms gleamed in the sunlight. Angelo headed straight toward them with his moped and disbanded them recklessly.

"Home you go, you old geezers!" he yelled.

The line of cyclists broke and scattered, and there was a chorus of curses shouted out at Angelo. I punched him in the back hard enough to take his breath away. He just laughed.

It was getting dark by now, so we stopped for a drink in a café. A café and milk bar in a god-forsaken little square, with an electric sign that attracted a nimbus of gnats. All around us were giant industrial buildings and a sports facility with an assortment of tennis courts. You could hear the *toc-tatunf* of the tennis balls and the whining drone of an electric circular saw. The café had tables outside, beneath a corrugated fiberglass awning. The radio was playing disco music from the seventies.

I will survive.

The barista came out to wait on us, a she-ogre in a miniskirt. Angelo ordered a whisky, and I asked for a fruit juice.

"Well, aren't we a nicely matched couple," he said, tossing down the shot of whisky as if it were fruit juice.

"I don't believe in couples," I answered, daringly, tossing back the glass of fruit juice as if it were a shot of whisky.

Angelo laughed, and then his face darkened. He can change moods as fast as a bee in flight can change direction. A group of dust-covered bricklayers, so-called alien workers, came into the bar.

They looked at us curiously, then began arguing among themselves.

"You want my woman?" Angelo suddenly shouted. They all turned to look.

"You want her? She's young, she's a little chubby, but she knows what she's doing."

"Shut up, you idiot," I said. "Sorry, he's drunk."

Angelo stood swaying and looking down at me with a dopey smile.

"Come on, boys, what are you afraid of? Sample the delights of Margherita Dolce Vita."

"Get out of here, you little shit," said a short bricklayer with a tired face.

I helped him out of the place; he was laughing and his eyes were rolling wildly.

"You happy now?" I hissed at him. "Nice little prank. Were you hoping they would beat you up?"

"Don't break my balls," he said. "I can take care of myself. And I carry a knife."

He showed me a little wooden-handled pocket knife, and he whirled it in the air.

"Blood is thicker than water," I said. "You like weapons, just like your dad."

He swallowed the insult in silence.

We returned home, zigzagging. He was singing, and I was holding on tight to him, but it wasn't the same.

Before, he was protecting me, now I was protecting him.

When we got back home, he had become docile again, as if

some phantom spirit had abandoned his body: his gaze had returned to normal.

"Well, that was an enjoyable outing in the lovely, toxic industrial hinterland," he said. "Look, we're covered with dust."

And he wiped off my mouth and forehead with his red bandanna.

"Listen, you animal," I said angrily. "I don't get you at all. You were almost human when you showed me the old folks on the balcony, then you start knocking people off their bicycles and trying to start fights in bars. Who are you?"

He looked at me, and I could only see his eyes and his dusty nose under the helmet. I suddenly understood.

Hannibal. It was my beloved Hannibal the Cannibal, wearing his muzzle. And he was a damaged, sick boy. And an angel. And an adolescent who had grown up too fast, and a shit, and my impossible love, and my next-door neighbor.

He was all these things at the same time.

"Angelo," I said to him, "let's play a game. Take off your helmet, let's pretend that we're still on the moped, and I'll climb onto the seat and wrap my arms around you."

He said nothing. I went ahead and did it, and he trembled.

I talked into his chest, without looking up at him.

"If I was three years older, and I weighed twenty pounds less, and my legs were longer and my ass was perkier and my tits were pointier and my ears were smaller and if I was rich and tanned and I had a greyhound on a leash and my name was really Daisy Sweetlife, well, with all this retouching, would you kiss me?"

"I would have to be crazy," he laughed.

He stroked my hair and my heart pounded so hard and I thought: *if he kisses me, I'll die.*

Unfortunately, he decided to let me live.

We pulled apart slowly, like a pair of amoebas, and I saw his face drain of color. The damned dark-blue car was arriving.

Frido got out; he was furious.

"I've told you a thousand times not to take Fedele's moped. You know that you can't drive in your condition."

"I drove perfectly well," he replied. He spoke without fear in his voice, or, for that matter, any emotion at all. His voice was dead.

"It's true, and we both wore helmets," I added.

"Keep out of this, Margherita, this is a family matter."

"We saw some beautiful graffiti," Angelo said, as if daring him.

"Beautiful to you. What did they paint this time?"

"See if you can find it. Don't tell him, Margherita."

"Shut up, you idiot," Frido said. "You were probably buying drugs from them."

"I'm not on drugs, Dad, you're on drugs."

Frido tried to slap him, but he dodged the blow. Fedele stood ready to step in.

"Get inside, or you go back to the clinic tonight. You reek of alcohol. You know perfectly well that you can't drink while you're taking that medicine. You want to kill yourself? Fine, try drinking just one more time."

Angelo looked at him with a ferocious glare. I thought about the knife and I was suddenly afraid.

"Angelo, please," I said.

"Get in the house!" yelled Frido.

"Go fuck yourself," said Angelo, and with a sudden lunge he leapt over the gate. I don't even know how he did it, he just grabbed the gate and flew over, as if he had wings.

Frido looked at me. His smile fled, but tatters of it caught somewhere, flapping feebly.

"It's just a passing crisis, but we know how to take care of him. Don't talk about this, if you don't mind."

"Of course not," I said.

"There are times when I wish I'd never had such a son," Frido sighed.

I went back to my house and closed the door to my room behind me. From Heraclitus's room, I could hear the voice of John Lennon. All the pain and grief in the world took a seat on my bed. The pain of Angelo the prisoner and my own pain. The weariness of the bricklayers. My mother's dissatisfaction, my father's anger, Giacinto's humiliated love. Frido's meanness, and the void inside Lenora, the weeping behind Labella's long eyelashes. The hopeless solitude of my grandfather. The breathing of the Dust Girl, concealed beneath the ruins.

All this will change, thought the knight, Sir von Opfwenderlingen.

The world is ancient, but in the era of the stars, it was still young, you have killed the childhood of the world.

In some distant hall in the castle, a bard was singing, while outside the window the first bats were on the wing.

The knight, Sir von Opfangelinden decided to set out for the field of battle.

When he arrived in the forest of Wartburg, he dismounted and removed his helmet.

And then it became clear that the fierce and greatly feared warrior was really just a young blond boy, only seventeen years old.

Come out, he said to the Dust Girl. I don't want to hurt you, and I'm not afraid of you.

And from the shadows of the tall oak trees, he saw two beautiful pale-blue eyes advancing toward him, terrible, the color of a winter sky.

Did I dream you dreamed about me?
Were you hare when I was fox?
Now my foolish boat is leaning
Broken lovelorn on your rocks,
For you sing:
"Touch me not, touch me not, come back tomorrow;
O my heart, o my heart shies from the sorrow"

I am puzzled as the newborn child
I am troubled at the tide:
Should I stand amid the breakers?
Should I lie with Death my bride?
Hear me sing:
"Swim to me, swim to me, let me enfold you;
Here I am, here I am, waiting to hold you"

The winter was blasting its cold winds of dire portent into the tender face of springtime. A chilly wind was killing the spring buds. Through the window of the schoolroom, I could see a big cloud. It changed continuously, stranding and tattering in vaporous gauze and then curdling into dense sculptures, metamorphosizing into sperm, curds, waves, and saliva, darkening and revealing an unsettling lightless core.

I was watching it from my school desk, and I was thinking to myself how many hours of my life I was spending in there. And yet, perhaps, one day I would think back on these hours and miss them.

One day, in a dream, I would hear the voices of my classmates behind a door. Maybe even the voice of our teacher, Mrs. Venturini, which was like a piece of chalk scratching across a chalkboard, and the racist ranting of Marra, and Zagarone as he slaughtered the songs of De André.

I was listening to my favorite teacher, my literature teacher. She was explaining that you don't say, *but however*, and that you also don't say, *and plus too also*. These are pleonasms. A pleonasm is the use of more words than necessary to express an idea, and she went on talking about pleonasms, talking and talking, and I thought to myself: well, she is right, but plus too also at the same time however, while she's explaining to us that we shouldn't use more words than necessary to make a point, she was using an incredible number of words, but however she didn't seem to notice.

There are times in life that are very "but however." The flow of events stagnates, and you can't tell in what direction things will finally move. And we drift through muddy waters. Then the water becomes clear, the river begins to flow quickly, and the water becomes crystal clear. And that was how my life was from that morning on.

I was floating in a deep pool of water, the last still water before the final rapids and waterfall. There, I could see what had been important in my life, my magnificent and tawdry childhood which was about to tumble into the void, everything that I would always love, even when it was far in the distance, long in the past.

I continued to mull over these thoughts in the jouncing school bus on the way home. Foreshadowed by a long, drawn-out, and menacing rumble of thunder, a cloudburst drenched down from the darkening sky just as the bus reached my stop and I stepped down into the street. It was about three hundred yards from the bus stop to my house: a long way for a twisted feeble heart like mine. I broke into a run. The rain was whipping down; I sang as I ran to keep up my spirits. I looked toward the forest and saw the treetops bending in the wind. I also thought I glimpsed Angelo, or someone who looked very much like him, standing stock-still in the middle of a field, like a scarecrow.

I turned into our yard with my heart in my throat, and a flash of lightning lit up my house, transfiguring it into Dracula's castle. Flocks of leaves torn loose by the wind flapped everywhere. The thunderclaps followed one after another; Zeus was pounding on the cosmic drums. Even the mega-Cube, in that giant maelstrom of unleashed forces, seemed nothing more than a tiny die cast into a puddle. The terrifying Bozzo was yelping with fear like a poodle. Along the rain-flooded road, lines of cars were honking their horns help-lessly.

Little house of mine, take me in your arms!

Sleepy ran frantically toward me, drenched and muddy, lit-tle more than a giant Martian mouse.

I was about to wash him off when he suddenly went rigid before my eyes; his legs lanced straight up in the air, and his whole body was as stiff as a board. The notorious meteoro-logically induced psychosleep-o-lepsy coma.

Now the mud is going to solidify on his body, I thought. And he will become a statue of a mongrel runt.

I'll set him on the windowsill with the inscription:

> SLEEPY THE GREAT,
> A NOBLE LITTLE BASTARD,
> EXEMPLARY AND LOYAL DOG,
> HE BRIGHTENED THE LIVES OF ALL WHO KNEW HIM.

Towards evening, everything was damp and grey. None of the stars were out. Not Sirius, not Carmilla, nor Dandelion.

I had gone to bed early, but I couldn't seem to fall asleep. Not even Pontius helped to calm my anxiety. My heart was doing a tango-step interspersed with a series of odd little *ta-ta-tunf* sounds, which I could feel in my throat and my tem-ples. By midnight I was wide awake. And then I heard a noise on the window glass, as if someone had thrown a pebble.

I opened the window and leaned out.

In the dark of the Del Benes' yard, I could barely make out the forms of Angelo and, at his feet, Sleepy, who had some-how made his way through the hedge. Angelo had something in his hand, and he seemed to be trying to show it to me; I couldn't make out what it was. Then he placed his index fin-ger across his lips and spread out both arms. I understood what he was trying to convey: I can't talk to you right now, but we'll meet at the tree of the cross.

"When?" I whispered loudly. He answered in a thin, reedy voice, "Tomorrow night at eight." Just then, the lights in the Cube came on, and he slipped away, Sleepy at his heels.

I went back to bed. It all seemed like a dream. Had I really seen them, or were they just phantoms? Just then there was a knock at my door. It was Heraclitus and Sleepy, and they were definitely flesh and blood. My brother had a strange expression on his face. He was very pale, and I noticed that wispy facial hair was beginning to sprout on his face. He had aged in just a few days, it seemed.

"Heraclitus, why are you up at this time of night?"

"I just can't seem to sleep. Come on, let's dance."

And he put on "I Am the Walrus" at full volume.

"Have you lost your mind? It's midnight."

He came close to me, with a sheet of paper in one hand, and whispered in my ear:

"Special agents Sherlock Heraclitus and Sleepy Watson, reporting for duty. The sound of the music will cover what we say. You were right. Something very disturbing is going on here. I understood when you showed me the mini-video camera in the ceiling."

"I've been aware of them for a while. That's how they knew everything that we were thinking and all the things we liked! How do you think they managed to install them?"

"The technician who put in the air conditioning system. He must have installed them. Do you remember how he climbed up on a ladder and pretended to be checking who knows what? They are the latest generation of spy cameras, Bugbear model. We can't let them figure out that we know about them. This is a map of where each camera is located, and the areas that they cover. I've spent the past three days identifying all the cameras. There aren't any in your bedroom, but there could be a listening device."

"So we have to listen to the music this loud?"

"Look, we are at war. The other night, I watched them through Grandpa's spyglass. Around eleven o'clock, Frido and Fedele went outside and started digging holes in the yard. Some guy in a ski mask joined them. I think it was Dad. They were in a far corner of the yard, and I couldn't get a good look at what they were doing. They dug for about half and hour and then left. Right after, I saw Angelo go and inspect the hole they had dug. Then Sleepy showed up from someplace, and started digging in the dirt. Look what he found . . . "

Heraclitus held out a small wristwatch, encrusted with clay.

"That's my wristwatch! The one I lost last year. How do you think it wound up over there?"

"Our investigation will attempt to answer that question."

"You're going to investigate, Heraclitus?"

"From this moment forward, you may call me Sherlock. Sherlock Erminio Holmes. Let's make a list of the things we know:

1. Our neighbors moved out here, but they don't seem to have been very happy about the idea.

2. Our neighbors are spying on us with tiny video cameras.

3. Every night, they dig strange holes in their yard, and our dad may be helping them.

4. Sleepy found your old watch buried there, the watch you lost a year ago.

5. Grandpa, who had been spying on them with his telescope, was badly injured in a hit-and-run motorcycle accident; you were almost ripped to shreds by Bozzo.

6. Dad has become Frido's business partner in a mysterious import-export company; he's filled the shed with crates, and he claims that they are artificial limbs, but he has forbidden us to enter the shed.

7. Frido is claiming to own a video game that does not exist.

8. Dad now owns a pistol that fires blanks (I know how to rummage through dresser drawers too, you know).

9. Four more cubes have been built in our neighborhood.

10. Lenora passes herself off as your aunt.

11. Darko has disappeared.

12. Angelo knows something that he wants to tell us.

13. But Angelo doesn't cast a shadow, and there are strange scenes in the windows of the Cube.

14. Somebody is trying to evict Pietro the farmer, so that they can build something on his land.

15. My math teacher either wears support hose or a garter belt.

The final result of the equation is:

> *Boogeyman, boogeyman, boogeyman, boo!*
> *Is this all a game or is it true?"*

"Well, none of makes any sense to me either, Heraclitus. But what does point 15 have to do with anything?"

"It's something I've been wondering about a lot lately."

"I understand. But I suggest we narrow our field of inquiry."

"Right. Sleepy Watson, do you have anything to add?"

"*Wo-o-off,*" said Sleepy.

"All right then. Let's turn off the music and go back to bed."

"I'm not sleepy," said Heraclitus. "Let's go see if we can find Dad's bottle of whisky."

"Heraclitus, you've never drunk alcohol in your life . . . "

"Well, maybe it's time to start," he said with a sigh.

I looked at him sharply. He had changed too, just as Grandpa had feared. His voice was hoarse, and his gestures were nervous and rapid, just like our father when he is trying to hide something. As if he had sensed what I was thinking, he said, "We can't waste a lot of time on myths and ghosts.

They are trying to do something bad to us, they want to hurt us. We need to defend ourselves. Dad has become a bastard."

"Heraclitus, such language . . . "

"A bastard who, like anyone who thinks they're powerful, hates us," he said in a low voice.

"Come on, Heraclitus, cut it out. What if your math teacher heard you talking?"

He grinned. I sensed he was about to say something vulgar. It dawned on me what he looked like, with the new hint of a mustache and his malevolent expression. He looked like a slightly diabolical plaster garden gnome. Sneaky, the Eighth Dwarf. I was about to tell him, but just then we heard a noise coming from the big shed. There were thudding blows, and the sound of something shattering.

The noise continued for half an hour. Then someone left the shed, and silence returned.

I didn't sleep at all, of course. Luckily, the next day was Sunday, and I could sleep in and laze around all I wanted. Plus, I was alone in the house.

My dad was away with Frido, Mamma had gone grocery shopping with Lenora, at the supermarket that doesn't finance illegal activities (and is instead owned directly by the Mafia). Giacinto was taking Labella to Glamglam, a very fashionable bar where she would flirt with every other guy in the house, and he would sink into a morass of thwarted love and low-alcohol beverages like the Bacati Squeezer, the Lemon Scramlizz, and the Orange Perversion.

I had the entire field of investigation lying open before me. If they were going to spy on us, then we should take up the challenge and spy on them in turn. Heraclitus had mysteriously vanished. I checked his chart of the surveillance system. His slanting, childish handwriting had stiffened into a strict geometric grid. I noted the places where there were no video cameras. For instance, in the little sheet-metal shack, next to the shed.

That's where my dad keeps his tools. If I find a shovel that's muddy or shows signs of recent use, I thought, then it was my father in the Del Benes' yard the other night.

I walked over to the tool shed with complete nonchalance. In fact, I said in a loud voice, "Well, since I have nothing else to do, maybe I'll get out a rake and rake up some fallen leaves."

It only occurred to me afterward that this might not be the best thing to say in springtime.

I went into the storage shed and turned on the light.

The shovel was there, covered with damp clumps of dirt and tufts of Astroturf.

But there was worse.

I noticed, on one of the higher shelves, a black box that I had never noticed before. It was locked.

I know that my dad keeps all his keys in the same place: beneath a plaster gnome, a headless Grumpy.

I said, "Pardon me, Grumpy," and lifted the gnome. In fact, underneath, there was a shiny new key, small and golden.

I opened the lid and . . .

Inside the box was a pistol. A long, shiny gun, the kind you'd see in a three-murders-a-minute movie, with a silencer and bullets that glittered like gems in the red-velvet lined case. On the same shelf, I found a pamphlet. I tucked it hastily into my pocket because I heard a noise outside. I stepped out of the shed, holding my little rake and with my most ingenuous expression on my face.

It was Mamma, staggering under a load of groceries.

"Give me a hand with this," she said.

I helped her to carry the shopping inside. There were more luxury items than even unnecessary items. There were more deodorants than loaves of bread, two pounds of hair rollers and only one pound of zucchini, and more wrinkle cream than mayonnaise. And she had forgotten to buy dog biscuits for Sleepy. CelluSlimmex causes memory loss. I helped her to put the food away in the refrigerator; then she immediately flopped down in front of the giant-screen television. I went into the bathroom and locked the door behind me. And I sat down to read the pamphlet.

RAGE OF GOD

CHURCH OF THE WRATH OF THE LORD

MARINES OF CHRIST — CENTER-NORTH BATTALION

PRESIDENT, K.K. KLANCY

Believers and citizens,
Our church is only newly arrived in your country but it has already conquered hordes of followers and legions of adepts; our ranks are growing rapidly. Against the false and half-hearted, who are attempting to discount the Rage of God, we bear the sword of the true faith.

More than five hundred new members have joined us this month, five hundred new Marines of God. You will find a list of their names at the bottom of this page, along with the sums that they have donated to the cause. Because the Rage of God is not merely a refuge for your soul, it is also a shield that will protect your own legitimate interests. Place in our hands your courage and we will convert it into prayers and bullets; entrust us with your savings and we will shower you with wealth and power. Our church employs the finest marketing experts in the world, we run more than a hundred banks, and we will protect your assets against the sly tricks and greedy maneuvers of Communist and Jewish high finance. And there won't be any hired judges trying to stop us.

Because, in the words of our founder and prophet, James Phaldo Reilth:

Every prayer in the name of the true God
is a pistol pointed at the enemy's head.
Every talent that you donate, we will hammer
into sharp spears and sturdy shields.
Those who scorn God will never know Him,
those who scorn money will never possess It.

But I wish to speak especially to you, Marines of Christ of this city.

This part of the world has long been a breeding ground for heretics and enemies of order. For many years the smoke of the bonfires with which heretics were burnt at the stake darkened the sky. For some time now, however, the battle for the true faith has waned.

Filthy subversive ideas and the lies told by feeble, homosexual false Catholics have allowed Lucifer to win back dominion over these lands.

But the sword of the Warriors is leveled at the throats of these infidels.

Forgiveness is the cowardice of the false warriors for Christ.

God has everyone in His crosshairs.

The hour of redemption is nigh. Pay no mind to those who call us a sect. We are a large and close-knit family, we have supporters and adepts in the

American government and in the government of this
nation. They are our friends and allies, but we are
stronger even than they, for the sword of the true
faith cannot remain concealed within the sheath of
politics.

Soon we shall build a new compound in this
city, with a church, auditorium, business consult-
ing center, and fitness rooms. We are working to
identify the best and cleanest neighborhood.

Come join us, and never forget:

According to the Third Bible, before Christ
died on the Cross, He killed thirty soldiers and
twelve judges. The blood on His brow was not His
alone!

Fight at our side, don't let them intimidate
you!

Mamma mia, I thought. My father, a member of a secret
sect of religious fanatics? My dad, who would go to Mass only
so that he could inspect the bicycles parked outside the
church? I could not believe this was happening. Just then,
Sleepy appeared, wagging eagerly.

There was a folded piece of paper in his mouth.

*Meet me tonight at eight o'clock at the tree of the cross. I
need to tell you something very serious.*

Angelo

Wow, I thought, this is some adventure. I stroked Sleepy's
pterodactyloid muzzle. He whimpered strangely, as if he were
trying to tell me something. If only I had known . . .

T he night that was to change my life began with a series of strange signs that I can properly connect only now. Dad spent the whole afternoon locked in the shed. We kept hearing those dull banging thuds, and there was an acrid smell in the air.

When Dad emerged, he acted wary. He was wearing camo pants and fishing boots. But he carried neither a fishing rod nor a net, or any of the other usual equipment for battling the wild trout.

I was in the field picking daisies when I saw an unusual gust of wind billow across the sea of grass. It was a hot dry gust of wind, a wave of dragon breath, pushing a cloud of poplar pollen, a blizzard of tiny phantoms.

The butterflies were fleeing, as if something was chasing them. And the woods shivered as if with fever.

Dust Girl was angry.

There was a great bustle of activity around the Cube; cars were driving in and parking in the rear. We couldn't see who got out.

I noticed Labella talking on the phone as she leaned against the gate; it looked like she was crying. I waved to get her attention, but she ignored me.

Every once in a while Frido or Lenora would appear, smiling, at one of the Cube's windows; a strong sense of deja-vu accompanied each apparition. Now he's going to kiss her on the forehead, I thought. And he did.

An idyllic vignette of family life. Then something changed. The window closed, and when it opened again, there were Robin and Mary Lou kissing, with a skyscraper in the background.

I ran inside, yelling for my mother: "Mamma, run, come see! 'Eternal Love,' live!"

By the time we got back, though, the window looked normal again. You could see the living room of the Cube, and Fedele dusting a chandelier.

But the most upsetting sign was the disappearance of Sleepy. He had failed to come home for lunch at one, or even later in the afternoon. It was a beautiful day, so he couldn't be in a storm-induced coma. He had never been gone for this long. Toward evening I started getting worried, and I told my mother.

"Maybe he's met some little bitch," she suggested with a dreamy air. She seemed drugged. Maybe those cellulite pills contained hallucinogens?

I wanted to talk to her, but she went into the kitchen and put some frozen French fries in the stove.

My astonishment froze me.

Mamma's fried potatoes were always the epitome of her cooking. When she would carefully peel the yellow potatoes and toss them into the pot, they seemed like a chorus of beautiful singers, harmonizing to the castanet rhythm of the sputtering hot oil. They were golden ingots, rare glistening gems, and their smell wafted throughout the house.

And she had always declared: frozen foods are for those who don't know how to cook; in episode one hundred fourteen of "Eternal Love," there is a panoramic view of the wicked Vanessa's refrigerator, fully stocked with frozen foods.

"Mamma, have you turned into a Vanessa?" I asked her.

"Lenora told me that the actress who plays Mary Lou does

advertisements for frozen foods. They keep you trim, they contain antioxidants, and they're not fattening."

"Mamma, you're not fat."

"I watched a fitness show yesterday. I did the finger test," she said, darkly.

"What's the finger test?"

"I stuck a finger into my thigh and it didn't bounce right back. That means I'm fat."

"Mamma, do you know which finger test I would try on the people who make shows like that on television?"

"Please, don't be vulgar. Leave me alone."

There wasn't much I could do now. She believed Lenora and the mega-screen more than she did her own eyes and her wise young daughter.

I wandered aimlessly through the house.

Giacinto was out somewhere. He was probably riding around on his moped, looking for his vanished Labella.

The eighth dwarf, Sneaky, was in his room with the door closed.

Sleepy was *desaparecido*.

I was alone.

So I sat down and read a book: *The Silence Before the Battle*, by Amlison Ynventemay.

Where she knows that he may kill her, but she goes to the rendezvous in the woods all the same.

With that remarkable scene where she, slender and agile, leaps onto the horse and gallops off across the steppe and goes to free him from the castle where he is being held prisoner by the evil sorcerer Prozac.

And that other scene of crazed, passionate sex . . .

Okay, you guessed it: there is no such book as *The Silence Before the Battle*, but I had some time to kill, so I made it up.

At seven-thirty I was getting ready for my rendezvous with Angelo and destiny.

"Where do you think you're going?" asked my father, appearing suddenly in a pair of colonel's uniform trousers, arms akimbo.

"I'm going to look for Sleepy in the fields," I answered, and it was half true.

"You can't go out, Margherita," he said sternly. "We've installed a new alarm system around here, concealed in the grass, and we haven't finished fine-tuning it. You might trigger the system and . . . "

"And then what would happen?

"The police would descend on the house, sirens would go off, and everybody would notice. This new work we're doing is secret and sensitive. This evening, you have to stay at home."

"Dad, I can't. I have to look for our dog . . . "

"Dogs come home on their own," my father opined. "Or else, if he's dead, best not to find him."

"The first rule of modern warfare is not to show the corpses," I said.

Dad pretended he hadn't heard me.

"Emma," he said brusquely to my mother, "I'm going back out to the shed. Make sure that Margherita stays at home. I absolutely forbid her to go out. Did you hear me? That's an order!"

Mamma didn't answer. Her gaze didn't veer from the mega-screen.

My dad flew into a rage. He walked over to her and grabbed the remote control out of her hand. He threw it to the ground. That's how we tested the protective rubber case.

"Christ, Emma, stop sitting in front of that TV and listen to me. Otherwise the smack I gave your daughter the other day will be yours today!"

In normal times, my mother would have answered him in

the same tone, and we would have been able to watch a nice knock-down fight, live. But if my father was flaring like a wooden match, my mother was flat, spent. She did nothing more than nod.

Colonel Fausto went out, slamming the door behind him. My dad, or the creature that had taken his place.

"Mamma," I said, "you can't let him treat you like this."

She made a tired gesture, and for a moment I could see my dear old used-up teabag of a mother. Then she said in a melancholy voice, "Work has him on edge; what can I do about it? Mary Lou says in episode three hundred thirty: 'how can we fight for what we want when the whole world is set against us?'"

"But she fights for her man Robin, and she wins."

"Only for a short time," Mamma sighed. "Lenora told me that she's already seen the second series. In episode nine hundred sixty-four, Robin leaves Mary Lou for a twenty-year-old intern. What's the point of suffering?"

"So that's why you're so depressed. Mamma, how can you go on believing what Lenora says?"

"She has so much more money than we do," Mamma said. "She can see the episodes directly by satellite."

"But life is not a soap opera, Mamma."

"No, it's worse, much worse."

I left her there, smoking her umpteenth virtual cigarette. Zapping frenetically from Carabinieri to comedians, idiots on reality shows and celebrity talk shows. Everything you could imagine. Except intelligence and talent.

Of course, nothing would keep from leaving the house. By now I know where the surveillance devices were located. So I used an old trick I had seen in a movie. I ran water to fill the tub, with a nice loud splashing roar. Then I recorded on my little tape recorder this lovely song, words and music by Margherita Dolce Vita:

Love Soaked
(Drenched with love for you)

I was like a sponge,
Light and carefree,
But I drank up your love
And my heart grew soggy.

Then I set it to "loop," so it would play hundreds of times in a row.

I went out the bathroom window with an agile leap, spraining an ankle as I landed. Behind me, I heard my own voice singing *Love Soaked*. Perfect. A light drizzle was falling, and a damp veil was covering everything, so that I was able to sneak away unseen.

I reached the tree of the cross, but Angelo wasn't there. I waited awhile, numb with the cold. There was a strange odor, something like resin. The cherry plum trees glowed like flames against the grey sky. At eight-thirty I admitted to myself that he wouldn't be coming, that something had happened.

The knight Sir von Opferdlingen heard the sound of the galloping knights coming to capture him.
I will never return to that dark dank dungeon, he thought to himself.
He spread his wings, to appear larger.

The cold enveloped me. I thought I saw shadows moving

among the trees along the river bank. I decided to venture
out.

The river had aged faster than I had over the winter. Pollu-
tion of all sorts had turned it into an Acheron of vomit. It
bore the spittle and various offenses of humanity. The water
was filthy with slobber and foul patches. Bobbing along it
were packing crates, plastic medusas, monstrous toy dolls,
and fish floating belly up.

And frogs as puffed up and fat as captains of industry,
croaking loudly.

Only a few years before, we used to come down to this river
to fish with our hands. And in summertime, we would walk
around in it hip-deep. Right here, for example, there was a
deep pool where a giant golden carp that we named Cleopatra lived.

And over there . . .

I heard a rustling in the leaves. A small shadow moved not
far off.

"Sleepy, is that you?" I said.

I carefully drew closer.

It was a big old female sewer rat, drenched and ferocious,
glaring at me with her beady malevolent eyes.

I'm not afraid of mice, but this was the Mother of All Rats,
and she was glaring at me with clear hostility.

I made a stab at diplomacy.

"Madame," I said to her, "I understand that you are angry
because I am trespassing in your home, and especially because
I gave you no time to tidy up. But let me assure you that I will
leave immediately."

She turned rapidly, whipping her tail as she went, and
allowed me to go on living.

Immediately after that experience, I stepped on a toad,
which zipped away from me like a rubber ball.

Then a mosquito flew up my nose.

And then a great big moth decided to inspect my hair.

I understood that I was the target of an attack of the river creatures, so I went back to the clearing where the tree was.

And then I realized what that odd smell had been.

It wasn't resin; it was the smell of a candle. And in fact I found on the grass a candle end; the wax was still warm. On the ground in front of the tree there were footprints, and a small depression, as if someone had knelt down there. I inspected the ground more carefully, and saw other foot-prints, as well as what looked like drag marks.

A broken branch, the leaves ripped off.

A long bird's feather, a plume.

I imagined an unpleasant scene. I tried not to picture it, but the film wouldn't stop rolling.

Angelo arrives, overwrought, with his dark secret and, as he waits for me, lights a candle at the foot of the tree.

Somebody arrives and drags him away, by force. Angelo struggles, he grabs a branch and rips away the leaves.

A feather falls from his wing.

My heart was racing crazily. I had to lie down in the grass.

And there, hidden from view, I saw them arrive.

They were the seven horsemen of the apocalypse.

Leading the pack was Frido, in camouflage overalls, with a gun dangling heavily against his tummy, possibly a subma-chine gun, I couldn't be sure. He was restraining Bozzo on a leash, and the dog was puffing and sniffing eagerly.

Behind him came a fat man with a beard and a cowboy hat. He didn't seem very fond of nighttime strolls; he cursed and stumbled at each step. Slung over his shoulder was a hunter's double-barreled shotgun. I instantly recognized Nevio Gaspar-rone, wholesaler of paints, and the father of my evil schoolmate.

Third in the line was Fedele Heitzmeesh, marching heavily, armed with his usual cell phone, combat boots, and, on his back, a rucksack filled with either hand grenades or snacks.

Fourth came a tall individual wearing a ski mask, whose pear-shaped silhouette clearly identified him as Piergiuseppe Garzoni. He was holding a carbine pointed dangerously at Fedele's ass, and coughing every so often.

Behind him came my father, wearing a huntsman hat with a pheasant feather, wading boots, and his holstered pistol. He looked like Heraclitus dressed up as a sheriff for Halloween.

Walking next to him was Giacinto, in soccer hooligan get-up, wearing a bomber jacket and carrying a baseball bat. He was even wearing a bandanna, the jerk.

Last in the line was Gordon the technician, very elegant in a policeman's uniform, though I don't know if it was real or just a costume. He was smoking as he walked and from time to time, he would turn to look behind him, to see if the daring little platoon were being followed.

There they were, the seven whoremongers of the apocalypse, marching toward who knew what warlike deeds, pre-emptive military operations, or intelligently administered beatings, and I didn't know whether I should laugh at their clumsiness or be frightened.

From the ranks came the sound of a fart, and Frido said sternly, "Silence, the enemy is listening."

Then I heard them snicker, and one of them exclaim, "There'll be a good old eviction tonight!"

They were heading for the fields of Pietro the farmer.

I thought that I should run and get around ahead of them to warn Pietro.

But I couldn't do it. My heart had derailed. It was beating so hard that I couldn't breathe.

Help me, sister Polverina, I was screaming inside, help me, stars.

Somebody placed a hand lightly on my forehead and I fainted.

When I recovered consciousness, it was no longer raining. I walked slowly home. It was almost one o'clock. Mamma was fast asleep in front of the mega-screen; she hadn't noticed a thing. Heraclitus instead was wide-awake, scared, and pushy.

"Where's Sleepy? Where have you been? Why are you so pale? What is that idiot song playing in the bathroom? What's happened?"

"One thing at a time, Heraclitus."

I told him everything I had seen. As I talked, my heart seemed to right itself and to return to the tracks.

"It's all becoming clearer," said Heraclitus. "Come on, let me show you something."

On the wall of the Cube, there was a slight glow.

"That is the glow of pixels. Those aren't windows. They're rear-projection screens. They are trying to hide what's really happening in that house, and they're putting out fake images to deceive us."

So Angelo hadn't been joking!

"Therefore," said Heraclitus, "the problem is mathematically rather simple, but it leads to two very different solutions:

a) either the Del Benes are a bunch of bizarre eccentrics who get a kick out of meddling in other people's affairs and playing war games and simulation games; or else

b) the Del Benes are a band of dangerous criminals, and Dad and Giacinto are their accomplices; maybe Mamma, too.

Given that, believing in possibility a), planet earth has afforded carte blanche to all sorts of criminals and destroyers, I opt for possibility b) and I officially declare war."

"Heraclitus," I said. "Let's not leap to conclusions. We're just kids, what can we do?"

"If the grown-ups haven't rebelled, we'll have to do it. History is looking down on us; I wouldn't want to make History throw up."

"I'm scared, Heraclitus. Tell me that it isn't true."

He looked at me. He had the determined expression of an adult. It seemed as if he had a Virtual cigar clenched between his teeth.

"Think about Sleepy, Margherita. Do you think you'll ever see Sleepy again?"

"Oh, yes."

"No, we won't see Sleepy again. Think carefully, Margherita. When did you lose that wristwatch?"

"A year ago."

"Where? Were you playing with Darko by chance?"

"Now that you mention it, maybe I was. I lost it after a soccer game, in the meadow."

"Darko was a good guy, but he was a thief. He stole one of my jackknives, dozens of soccer cards, and a photo of my math teacher naked."

"Heraclitus!"

"It was something I did with Photoshop. But do you understand what I'm trying to say?"

"You mean that . . . "

"That Sleepy did some digging in their yard and that he found the watch because he found Darko. Or what was left of Darko. Please, don't faint."

"It's all too horrible," I said, in the grip of a new systolic derailment. "Just leave me a little hope, Heraclitus."

"No. Don't try to call horror by a different name. That's their job."

"Grandpa Socrates," I said, "is that you talking? Are you communicating?"

"I'm old enough to do my own talking," Heraclitus said brusquely. "The key to the whole mystery is in the shed."

He was calm and decisive. A person can become a general or a tyrant in a single day.

"Read this," I said, and I gave him the Rage of God flyer.

"I know about them," said Heraclitus. "Yesterday Dad told me that they're a bunch of clowns. It seemed as if he were making a special effort to tell me how much he hates them."

"Did you believe him?"

"There is no sect so stupid and bloodthirsty that it can't find followers. For years, I was a member of a sect called the Playpigs; we specialized in finding codes to undress the heroines of video games. Giacinto used to be a member of Belzeballs, a satanic/athletic sect that performed soccer-ball sacrifices and burned soccer cards. Mamma is a member of the 'Eternal Love' Fan Club. Dad used to belong to the APECP, Association for the Preservation of Enameled Chamber Pots. Grandpa Socrates was the chairman of the Mermaid Worshipers' Society, a sect that would collect sightings of fish-women, and organize orgies with girls in wading pools."

"Horrors!"

"Horrors indeed, but there are camarillas and cabals that are far worse, though none half as bad as the clique of the Seemingly Normal. We need to get inside that shed and find out what's in there. And it won't be artificial legs and prosthetic limbs."

"How do you know?"

"I saw them unload that semi trailer. It took a forklift, and at least three people, to move one of those crates. Prosthetic limbs don't weigh that much."

"When do we go?"

"Tomorrow night. 3 A.M. sharp. Dress accordingly. Now hush. They're back, do you hear them?"

We heard car doors slamming. Then we saw the whore-mongers of the apocalypse bidding each other goodnight with jovial backslaps of complicity. Someone loaded a large bag into a car.

Dad and Giacinto came walking down the driveway. They were striding along and singing:

> *Run, rabbit run, I'll still catch you all right,*
> *And a fire will be burning tonight*
> *Ta-tunf ta-tu tunf.*

They went into the shed. Again, we heard the dull thuds and smelled the acrid aroma.

Soon we'll know everything.

21. BATTLE PLAN

We had a well-thought-out plan, and the first move that morning was to act naturally and keep from attracting notice.

I brushed my teeth, singing like a nightingale.

Heraclitus gave Mamma a good-morning kiss.

I opened the door that led to the backyard and said, "What a shitty day!"

It was drizzling as usual in this depressed spring. Everything was normal. The sky was a dull ravine-yellow.

The last deep, still pool before the water began to roar over the edge and into the void.

At school, I talked to everyone with nonchalance; I even accepted a piece of candy that Zagara offered me. He asked, "You want to go out some evening?"

"Zagara," I replied, "if you want to lure a young girl with candy, you need to be at least fifty years older than you are."

Then, moderately interested, I listened to the teacher talking. I nodded along with the lesson, like one of those bobblehead dogs that people used to put on their rear dashboards. What ever happened to bobblehead dogs? And hula-hoops? And Teenage Mutant Ninja Turtles? And flypaper? And democracy?

I needed to keep from daydreaming, so I used an old trick. I took my Greek lexicon, put it on my chair, and sat on top of it. The corners hurt your ass, so you stay wide awake and keep from drifting off. The only thing is that you look like you're six feet tall.

Everything was fine until the break. La Baciolini asked me, "Have you heard what happened near your house?"

"No," I said, my heart in my throat.

"You remember Pietro, the farmer that used to sell apricots along the road?"

"Yes?"

"They found him dead in his shack. He fell and hit his head. Apparently, he drank like a fish."

"Who told you that?"

"Garzoni. His father told him about it. He must have been delighted, just imagine, more land where he can build those huge apartment towers."

I could hardly breathe, but I managed to make it to the end of the lesson without twitching a single facial muscle. Margherita the Sphinx.

When I got home, I smiled at Dad, Mamma, and Giacinto.

Dad and Giacinto seemed happy; they were playfully punching one another: there was a new complicity between them. I was jealous. You can be jealous even of monstrous things.

"Giacinto has become a man," my dad said proudly.

"Even if he has become a Dynamo fan?" I asked.

"Dynamo is a winning team," snarled the earring-wearing turncoat. "And I'm tired of having my team lose all the most important matches. I want to come in first. I want to get ahead in life. You just keep on composing your little idiot poems."

"You don't want even one little poem to win Labella's heart?"

"Labella has gone away to boarding school and I don't give a damn about the little slut," said Giacinto.

But beneath the blatting trombone of cynicism, I could hear the despairing violin of lost love.

At lunch, there was an unexpected air of merriment. Mamma seemed livelier. Heraclitus had stolen her cellulite pills and hidden them. A hefty meatloaf appeared on the table.

"No news about Sleepy?" asked my dad, in an unruffled tone of voice.

"Please," I said, "don't talk about Sleepy in the presence of the meatloaf."

"Of course not," said my dad. "Your mother and I are monsters, we'd kill our own dog and grind him up and put him in the meatloaf. Or bury him in the garden. By the way, did you go out last night?"

"No, Dad."

"But an alarm did go off."

"You said it yourself, Dad. The system is new, it still has bugs. There must have been a malfunction."

"Technology doesn't make mistakes," Dad said self-importantly.

Right then, with his mouthful of food, his cheeks puffed out, and his toupee neatly combed, he seemed just like Frido's twin.

That afternoon, I didn't know what to do with myself. I watched my parents and Giacinto, and I tried to remember how they used to be, in the days when I would look at them and understand what they were thinking. I wish I wasn't afraid of them. It's a bad thing to be mistrustful at my age. It stays with you forever.

But they had changed. They weren't living anymore; they were waiting for someone to tell them how to live. Every gesture they made was different; it was as if they were in a hurry.

They no longer seemed to care about what they did. There was no attention, no gentleness in their actions.

And I remembered the way they used to be.

Dad fixing bicycles calmly, spinning the pedal and saying, "listen to that music."

Mamma coming back from the fields with a handful of radicchio and a nice bee-sting on her forehead.

Giacinto playing soccer with his friends in the meadow, with the resounding thumps of the ball being kicked, the loud belches and the laughter.

And then I remembered Grandpa too. When he would go out fishing and would still not be back by lunchtime. We would find him fast asleep under a tree, with a catfish that had been hooked for three hours, swimming idly as if to say: look, either reel me in or let me go.

And Sleepy curled up, eyes closed, drinking in a shaft of sunlight.

Was all this lost forever? Was it inevitable that it would change? Should I just try to forget it? Should I close my eyes to it? Should we try to forgive, because each of us lives on the crumbs that life offers? Should we think that all our troubles are just tiny things as seen from the distant stars, from Althazor, Grapatax, Mab, Zelda, and Dandelion? Or else, precisely because we are little, shouldn't we fight for our tiny crumb of justice, lest the stars themselves fall from the sky?

My appointment with Heraclitus was at three in the morning, and I needed to stay awake. But I hadn't got much sleep the night before, and I nodded off. I dreamed the dreams of the rest of my family. Because if we understand the dreams of the others, I thought, maybe we won't be separated.

I entered my father's dream.

We were walking together in the meadow, and he was saying, "Margherita, I know that you're disappointed in me, but you just don't understand. I decided to change my own life, because I wanted something. *People have desires*, as your favorite philosopher Hannibal Lecter likes to point out. It's true, I went into business with that bastard Frido, and I joined that buffoonish sect, but it was all part of my plan to build a great dream, my old dream of restoring the souls of old objects. There is a surprise for you."

We had arrived at our home and . . .

Next to the Cube there was a pyramid. A genuine, very ancient Egyptian pyramid.

"Nice, isn't it? I had it dismantled and shipped here, stone by stone. It would have just been sitting in Egypt, no good to anyone except as a tawdry backdrop for some tourist's snapshots. Instead, here we can live in it, it can become our home. You will sleep in Nefertari's chamber. We'll have hieroglyphics in our living room. Sleepy will enjoy bones of incredible vintage. Wasn't it worth a few compromises to have all this?"

I entered my mother's dream.

She was elegantly dressed, at an "Eternal Love"-style cocktail party; through the windows you could see the skyscrapers of New York City; a few of them were pear-shaped. Frank Sinatra was playing at the piano-bar. Everybody was sipping Martinis and eating Botox hors-d'oeuvres. Standing next to Mamma was Lenora. Mamma was saying to her:

"Darling, forgive me if I say so, but those pointy-toed shoes really don't go with your suit. And your perfume, if I may say so, is *so* last year. Have you tried my *Eau de Sleepée*?"

Lenora gazed at her, boundless admiration in her eyes. Then a man walked into the room; he had Dad's face, Robin's physique, and a meatloaf-colored tuxedo.

"Emma," he said, "I finally understand: I'm crazy about you and I want to marry you."

"Too late," Mamma replied. "I'm getting married to Gordon, the television technician."

"Why?"

"I am sick of my old 21-inch husband. I want a 48-inch husband. You're an obsolete model, Robin, just go back to your bicycles and your sluttish interns."

I entered Giacinto's dream.

He had just returned home from a party where he had danced like a professional and beaten up just about all the guests. Labella was waiting for him in front of our house, drenched, in the pouring rain.

"Giacinto," she said to him. "You haven't answered any of my text messages in three days. Why?"

"Well, I've been pretty busy," said Giacinto, as he took off his overcoat. Underneath, he was wearing a uniform studded with ribbons and medals.

"You know, since I got back from that damned war, I've just felt like having a little fun."

"Oh, Giacinto," sighed Labella, "you look so fine in uniform. Can I come upstairs to your place?"

"Sure, but tomorrow morning you need to clear out early. I have a meeting with the board of the Nacional soccer team; after the championship we need to decide on our draft picks for next year."

"Kiss me," sighed Labella, melting into his arms.

"Affirmative," Giacinto answered, and passionately browsed her face.

I entered Grandpa's dream.

He was with his girlfriend Lupinda Gutierrez, and they were about to set sail on a cruise. They were waving at me from the deck of the cruise ship. Grandpa was wearing a necklace of poppy flowers around his neck; she was beautiful and diaphanous.

· "Margherita," he was saying, "if you need me, tell Heraclitus. And whatever happens, don't forget me. And write, write . . . "

I entered Heraclitus's dream.

He had been kept after school, and was sitting alone in the classroom with his math teacher. Miss Stork was sitting across from him, her long legs crossed. She was saying:

"Heraclitus, I kept you after because we need to talk. You see, mathematics is a complex science. I know the doubt that is troubling you, and I wouldn't be much of a teacher if I didn't help you to solve it."

Then she gave him an irresistible smile.

"Well, yes," she said. "I wear garter belts."

That day we read no further.

I entered Sleepy's dream.

He was in the middle of the meadow. Looming above him was a turd that towered nine feet tall, a totem pole, the anaconda of dog shit. Photographers and flies had come from all over the world.

"That's my friend," Bozzo was saying proudly.

"I did it," Sleepy was telling me, panting excitedly.

22. THE LAST NIGHT

Suddenly, I was dreaming about Angelo.

He was behind a door, I could hear him singing.

I called to him.

"Beat it," he was saying to me. "I don't want to be buried alive in there again."

"But it's me, Margherita," I shouted.

And then we were both sitting in a bathtub together.

And he kissed me.

Then suddenly I had woken up, my heart in my throat.

Something was happening in the Cube.

A window opened. But this time it wasn't a screen and it wasn't "Eternal Love." It was a real-life scene: Lenora was leaning out the window and screaming, while Frido was trying to pull her back in.

"You shouldn't have done it, not this, Frido!" she shrieked. "I accepted everything, but not this. Not our son, no!"

"Shut up, you madwoman!" he was yelling, and he jerked her back in violently by one arm.

"No, no!" she kept screaming. "Not my Angelo, it's all your fault . . . "

The darkness swallowed up her voice, and the window swung shut.

I ran downstairs. Mamma was on the couch in front of the mega-screen.

"Did you hear the screaming?"

"Um, yes," said Mamma without looking up. "It was the television. Someone was having an argument in a movie."

"No, Mamma," I said. "It was Lenora and Frido."

"It was the television, isn't that obvious?" said my dad, appearing at the kitchen door. "Go back to bed, Margherita."

I looked at my mother. She was glued to the sofa, with the bluish light of the devilish plasma screen on her face, her hair stiff with hairspray, her face pale and Botoxed.

I wanted my old used-teabag Mamma, with her wrinkles and her smiling eyes. I picked up the remote control, I pointed it at her, and I yelled, "I am pushing the rewind button, Mamma. This is an order: go back in time!"

She jerked suddenly, as if she had suddenly seen me for the first time, and she said, "Margherita, it's the most terrible thing. Lenora was crying into the telephone. She told me that something bad had happened to her son, then I heard Frido's voice and the line went de—"

She never finished the sentence.

Dad grabbed the remote control out of my hands and pushed the off button.

Mamma and screen both went blank.

I understood that there was nothing more that I could do. There was no alternative but to carry out our plan in full. We were alone.

"I won't close my eyes again," I said to myself. Instead, I fell asleep and dreamed of Angelo.

He was standing in the meadow, arms spread wide, as if he had been crucified. Barefoot, muddy, his hair drenched. But he was smiling.

"What are you doing?"

"Can't you see? I found a job. I'm working as a scarecrow."

"Shut up."

"For real! Pietro hired me. Look, here comes a crow now."

It wasn't a crow at all. It was Sleepy: he was beautiful, with two white stork's wings.

"Don't change the subject," I said. "You kissed me."

"The first and the last time," he said.

"Are you going away?"

"Maybe."

The meadow was crackling with the falling rain. Then in the sky I heard the noise of an airplane.

Angelo took my hand.

"I saw her," he told me, "She's beautiful, she touched me. She's not a ghost, she's not made out of dust. She is real, as real as the fact that we are here."

At three in the morning, the alarm clock with the Minnie Mouse ears (an old gift, a token of love) rang softly under my pillow, waking me up. I had gone to bed in overalls, with a flashlight in my pocket, and it only took me an instant to climb out the window. An agile leap and I was standing next to Heraclitus. The stars were glittering curiously, and the breeze bore a scent of damp grass.

Neither countryside nor city, neither desolate nor crowded, here we fought the last battle.

Heraclitus's face was even more serious than usual. He checked his chart of the alarms. We zigzagged for a little while, and then we began to crawl across the lawn until we reached the back of the shed.

"Are we crawling because there are electric eye beams?" I asked him.

"No, because this is how they do it in the movies," he answered.

In the back of the shed there is a little window. This was our secret entrance, from when we were little and we would sneak in with our friends to play. We would besiege Giacinto, barricaded inside Fort Frigidaire, behind a palisade of refrigerators. Or else we would climb into the old wardrobes to pretend we were in a bathyscape, to play hide-and-seek, or doctor and other such delights.

As we had done so many times before, we opened the little window from outside with a piece of hooked wire.

"Sure there's no alarm?" I asked Heraclitus.

"Almost certain. Come on, let's go in."

That was when we ran into our first problem.

Heraclitus climbed up onto an oil drum and slipped in through the window. I remembered that as a child I had climbed in easily, but that was many years and many pounds ago. I got stuck halfway through.

The stars looked down in astonishment at my little legs kicking in midair.

Finally Heraclitus pulled me through by one arm, and I scraped my bottom as I went.

How embarrassing.

We were in the dark, in a forest of old bicycles. My dad had stacked them all at the back of the shed. I saw Lady Legnano with an injured handlebar. She was sleeping.

For an instant, it all seemed like it was in the old days. The smell of mold, old wood, and dead dolls. It was still our old playroom. Every wardrobe concealed a secret, every broom was a witch's head, every shadow was a dinosaur. The smell was the same, the sound of our breathing was the same.

Come on, let's play again, Giacinto, Luisa, Lorenza, Erminio, I wanted to say.

Come play with us, Angelo.

And I heard a rustle. A wail. Or maybe it was just the wind, blowing through the little open window.

*

I switched on my flashlight and stood, open-mouthed.

Leaning against the wall were dolls of all sizes. Male and female mannequins, with fake hair in various colors. Even mannequins of children.

Their blank eyes stared at us, their arms were frozen in gestures of salutation, or mockery.

"That's why they had all these artificial limbs," Heraclitus explained. "They assemble them to make these."

"What do they do with them?"

Heraclitus pointed to a pile of dummies in a corner. Some of them had their chests torn open, others were missing a leg or an arm. One mannequin of a woman had been decapitated.

"They use them as targets," Heraclitus said. "They shoot them, to test some weapon or other. You see this? It's a bullet hole."

He was fiddling with the head in one hand.

"Put it down," I said.

In the middle of the shed were the crates, in neat rows of four.

"Let's open them," I said.

"You do it," said Heraclitus. "You're the manpower, I'm the mastermind."

"Thanks for the compliment," I said. "But won't we make too much noise?"

"We've already made plenty."

I picked up a metal bar, and I pried at the top of the crate with it. It opened easily with a screech and a shower of splinters.

Heraclitus leaned over and into the crate, head-first.

"Just as I thought," he said.

I looked in too. The crate was full of wonderful toys. Real rifles and Uzi submachine guns and pistols to shoot at redskins.

The second crate was full of jolly round landmines that vaguely resembled cow pies.

"Antipersonnel mines," Heraclitus explained. "Domestic production, I studied them on the Internet."

The third crate took more work to open.

It contained tubes of some shiny metal, with digital timers and keyboards. They looked like giant cell phones.

"Well, my goodness," said Heraclitus, "this is the real stuff: HUSB fragmentation bombs with remote control switches; they'll rip open an armored car like a can of tuna."

He started fiddling around with the remote control as if it were a PlayStation, at top speed.

"Be careful."

"I know all there is to know about these bombs. I have already used them in three separate video games. And there is a special website all about them on the Internet. Okay, all done."

"What's all done?"

"Nothing, I just wanted to check to make sure they worked. What do you say, shall we open more crates?"

"I think we already know too much," I said.

"Someone's coming," said Heraclitus. "Turn off the flashlight. Here we go."

23. The Challenge

The loud rattling roar of the front door being rolled up, like a metallic waterfall.

Moonlight poured in through the open door, and we saw the dark silhouettes of Dad, Frido, Giacinto, and Fedele.

Men without women, strong and well armed. The breed of the future. And the wail became a thin faint voice:

Are you getting closer? Have you come to save me?

"Why, what curious children," said Frido, stepping forward with a preemptive smile.

"It's not like you think, Margherita," said my dad in a calm voice.

"We're secret agents," said Giacinto.

"Shut up, you idiot," said Frido, and he continued to walk toward us.

"Stop right there," Heraclitus roared. "Or I'll pick up a bomb."

I had never heard him talk like this.

Frido stopped short.

"Don't do anything foolish, children. You have nothing to fear," he said.

"Then why do you have a pistol behind your back?" I shot back.

"We thought you might be burglars."

"Come on now," said Heraclitus. "If you are here now, you have certainly known for a while that we were here."

"Certainly," said Frido with a sneer, "the world of business isn't a video game for children. Did you think that we would have left the shed without alarms?"

"Well, we gave it a shot," said Heraclitus.

"I imagine that you are all astonished, and that you want an explanation," said Frido. "But I'll explain only once, and after that you'll forget about all this. Agreed?"

"We hear you loud and clear," I said.

Frido sat calmly on a crate, and set his pistol down on top of it.

"All right then," he began. "My company, DB International, develops and manages security systems."

"Security systems," my dad echoed him.

" . . . ystems," Giacinto trailed off.

"We work directly for the Ministry of Defense. We work on everything, antiterrorism systems, espionage, weapons technology. All of the most up-to-date developments."

"Though when you need to run down an old man, you just use an ordinary motorcycle," said Heraclitus with a strange, hoarse voice.

"I do not wish to be interrupted," said Frido, and cast a quick glance over at his pistol.

Heraclitus, in a flash, reached into the crate full of bombs.

No more weapons. At least not you, little brother.

"Let him explain," said Dad, with a quiver in his voice.

"Now then," Frido went on. "We installed miniature video surveillance cameras in your house to test a new system for monitoring terrorists. After the first few days of testing, of course, I informed your father."

"That's true," said Dad.

"As for these weapons, they were confiscated from illegal arms merchants, the Russian and Colombian Mafia, and so on. In this laboratory-shed we are storing the materiel that has been confiscated and we are investigating to determine origins and destinations. We are also doing ballistic testing with dummies, as you may have gathered. We are studying target impacts."

"How to blow up and kill people, in other words," I said.

"If you want an old-fashioned description, certainly, you could say that."

"And what do you do with the weapons?"

"We destroy some of them, others we hand over to the regular legal and judicial authorities. We do not sell them. Do you believe me?"

"Not entirely. I would have further questions," I said.

"Be my guest," said Frido. "Depositions, subpoenas, and judges have never frightened me."

"Why the Cube?"

"In the future, the Cube will become the basic architectural form used for military camps and other civilian targets that require special protection. We are testing twenty or so cubes in various sections of the city."

"Why don't you have any windows, only screens that project videos?"

"This is an invention that ought to interest you, Heraclitus, and if you like I'll show it to you. It's called FakeView. It's a new system that serves to conceal the activities taking place inside. It is a counter-espionage tool, it camouflages activities and creates false targets to deceive the enemy."

"What is 'Rage of God'?"

"It's a gang of morons who are playing soldiers. We are keeping an eye on them to make sure they don't do anything stupid."

"What were you doing patrolling down by the river the other night?"

Frido and Dad looked at one another, then Frido selected the most unconvincing laugh in his entire repertoire, practically a death rattle.

"Well, to tell the truth, we sort of played at being cowboys. We need to have a laugh every once in a while!" he sneered. "We went rat-hunting. We cleaned out the whole river. Rats breed diseases, the bastards."

"Fucking shitty rats," added Giacinto, with one of his old soccer hooligan sneers.

Heraclitus and I looked at one another.

"I didn't hear any shooting," I insisted.

"We used a silencer, little girl," replied Frido with an exasperated sigh. "We tried out the new Maruzen model. You can't imagine . . ."

"Maruzen 09, sound reduction by as much as thirty decibels, titanium chamber, fits .38 caliber handguns," said Heraclitus quickly.

"My goodness," said Frido. "You'll be one of us soon."

Heraclitus seemed flattered.

"And what else have you cleaned out?" I pressed. "Any annoying bipeds?"

Frido shot to his feet, knocking a dummy over with a loud noise. I could sense his rage from where I was, yards away.

I'm scratching the wall, do you hear me? There's not much air left.

"Certainly, Margherita. We have expelled Gypsies and graffiti artists, hoodlums and thieves without residence documents, and we will continue to do so. In this area, we are going to build a research and training center for new military technologies. Camp Pear. And Giacinto is the first to enroll. Any other questions, madame magistrate?"

"What happened to Darko?"

"Who?"

"You know perfectly well. That Gypsy friend of mine who used to wash windshields at the stoplight."

"I believe he was sent back to his own country, expelled by the police judge."

"What was my watch doing buried in your yard?"

"What watch?" asked Frido. This time he seemed surprised.

Giacinto took a step forward: this was his big moment.

"Hell, Margherita, you're really an idiot. Their backyard used to be the field where we would play soccer. That's where you lost it. Did you forget?"

"Good job, Giacinto," said our father. "Explain to your sister that she's talking nonsense."

Giacinto glowed in a soldierly manner.

For an instant I was tempted to just let it all drop, laugh it off, and say: all right, I've had it with this silly game. It's driving us all crazy.

But Heraclitus stepped between us, in front of me, legs spread, mimicking Frido's challenging stance.

"What happened to the farmer in his shack?" he asked.

"Dead of a heart attack, as stated in the coroner's report."

"Why are you digging holes in your yard?"

"We're installing a new model sensors for the alarm system."

"Where's Sleepy?"

This time our dad answered.

"Yesterday I saw Sleepy only a block away from here . . . quite busy with a little bitch. I'll bet you he'll be home any day now."

"So, as you put it, shall we call a truce?" asked Frido.

Boogeyman, boogeyman, boogeyman, boo!
Is this all a game or is it true?

Frido seemed relaxed. Cagey, manipulative, and relaxed. Dad was sitting down now, and he was running his fingers through his pseudo-hair. Giacinto was scratching his crotch. Fedele stood stock-still, a statue, arms folded on his chest. Everything seemed so normal. I looked over at Heraclitus. He had an inscrutable and completely grown-up smile on his face.

Frido began to walk toward us again.

"Now we can consider two different endings to the movie. You're smart kids, and you've already seen lots and lots of movies, good movies and bad ones. The first ending is that we're monsters. Your father and your brother, people you have known your whole lives, are murders and accomplices to murder. We are arms merchants, we operate a death squad, we run down eighty-year-old grandfathers in the street, we beat to death gypsy boys and innocent farmers, we strangle dogs, and then we bury the bodies in our backyard. But there's a different, more reasonable ending to this movie. Look me in the eyes, Margherita. It's true, I am a businessman and sometimes I can play hardball. But first and foremost I am a man who loves his country. I don't like people who want to disrupt law and order in my country. I don't like people who threaten us all with weapons. And the things I do, I do to defend you and your brothers. It's going to be a long war, but we are going to win it. Fear will be the single purest emotion for you in the years to come, Margherita. Learn to embrace fear. But with us to protect you, you'll be a little less afraid. Because we are developing new ways to defend ourselves, new security systems, a new kind of intelligence, a new industry to fight the enemy."

"Who is the enemy?"

"The enemy is whoever we say," answered Frido.

If I get out of here alive, I will run through the meadow, from one end to the other, until I drop dead from exhaustion, panting feverishly. I will forget, if I ever can.

*

Outside, the moon was hidden by clouds. By now the four figures were dim shadows, lost in the darkness of the shed.

"Trust us, Margherita," my father said. "Remember all the wonderful things we have done together. Move away from those crates; that stuff is dangerous."

"Please, chunky sister," Giacinto sniveled. "I'm your brother. You said it yourself, for love a person will do anything. I love Labella, I love my country, I love . . . "

"Dynamo?"

He glared at me with cold hatred in his eyes, and I noticed that he was armed like the others. Frido gestured to him to calm down.

"Come on kids, let's resolve this misunderstanding. I'm getting tired. So far we've been very patient with you, but enough is enough. It's a powder keg in here. Something could blow up any second. Either you leave peacefully, or we'll have to treat you pretty harshly."

"Just a minute," said Heraclitus. "Do you see this switch I'm holding? It controls a HUSB time bomb."

"You wouldn't know how to operate that thing," said Frido, turning pale.

"All you have to do is enter a seven-digit code and synchronize it with the code for the timer on the bomb, then you set the timer and enter your own three-digit personal code."

This time, Frido couldn't manage even a fake laugh.

"Fausto, what the hell kind of son do you have?"

"Erminio, I don't even recognize you . . . "

"And yet we never really resembled one another, Dad," said Heraclitus, his face barely visible in the dim light of the flashlight. "You've invented more powerful and sophisticated weapons, but you've also invented people who will figure out how to use them, both unprincipled bastards and well-behaved boys like me. Your weapons have a weak point.

Since you have to sell them, you have to sell the instructions to go with them. One day, an elementary school might become a nuclear power."

"Don't fool around with that remote control, Erminio," our father said. "Frido explained everything; why won't you believe us?"

The flashlight was fading. It became totally dark in the shed. I could scarcely make out my brother anymore: he had moved over against the wall.

"Sure, Dad," said Heraclitus, with the same hoarse voice. "Frido answered all the questions brilliantly. Like a colonel at a press conference, after an operation. The way they explain how different it is to be decapitated by a smart bomb, as opposed to a primitive dagger. Or why we should accept civilian deaths, or why torture is a necessary pastime. But you see, Dad, you have repeated these things so many times, with abbreviations and charts and discussions and statistics, and each time it becomes clear afterwards that you have lied. We understand that you aren't right, you aren't trying to reason with us, you're not playing fair: all you have is lies. New, sophisticated weapons, but old, age-old, crude lies. So we don't believe you anymore. We are walking out of your little death drama."

"So how do you want this to go, you little bastard?" asked Frido.

There was a moment's silence, broken only by an impossibly distant sound of music, like the flowing of a river. And that wailing lament:

Here I am, just inches away.

"Well, maybe, now that we've come to this understanding, we can all walk out of this shed and go our separate ways," said Heraclitus, suddenly calm. "But let's just check one last thing. Under the floor of this shed there's a trap door and an oubliette. Let's see if you have anything hidden under there. If it's empty, then we have all just been dreaming."

"A trap door? I didn't know anything about it," said Frido, looking over at Dad.

"I'd forgotten about it," said my dad. "It's just a space under the floor, full of dust and rubble. Sure, let's open it up."

"And no vendettas, afterwards," I added. Frido thought it over and made a rapid decision.

"I swear, no retaliation," he said, raising both hands in the air. "How could I take revenge against the children of my friend and business partner? I'm a father myself."

"Just one last question, Doctor Frido," I said. "Since you mention the fact that you're a father, too. Where is Angelo?"

"We'll see him soon," said Frido, and for once his voice quavered. "Come on, let's open up this mysterious trap door."

Something is always hidden from those who wish to hide.

Suddenly, there was a burst of noise. Rain had started rattling down on the roof of the shed. It sounded like the din of an ancient battle, with swords and shields.

"Giacinto can come help us, the rest of you stay there," said Heraclitus, who still had the remote control switch in his hand.

Giacinto came with us, clearly a little frightened. We moved a wardrobe aside, uncovering the slab of stone. It looked like it had been there for centuries; it was covered with cobwebs. There was an illegible inscription on it. Heraclitus and Giacinto began to force it open. I helped them.

"There's nothing of ours under there!" Frido exclaimed.

"Oh yes there is," said Heraclitus, just as the trap door creaked and began to inch open. But it wasn't us prying the slab open anymore. There was something inside, something enormous that was pushing to get out. There was a scream growing closer, and the walls of the shed began to vibrate. Giacinto went pale, Heraclitus shoved me away. The enormous heavy slab flipped into the air, turning as if it were made of paper, and the depths of the earth vomited up a black hissing specter, a cloud of dust swollen with gusting wind and anger, the scream that knows that it is the last scream in the world. I began coughing and groping in the dark.

"What's happening?" my father yelled.

"Daddy, help me!" cried Giacinto.

"I can't see anything, you bastards!" yelled Frido furiously.

I heard the sound of footsteps and curses. I tried to make my way toward the exit, while the trap door continued to vomit forth dust. The shed had become a dark and toxic inferno. But I knew every inch of that shed by heart, and I knew how to get out. I blundered toward the door, fingers feeling my way, until I gulped down a lungful of cool air and I understood that I was outside. Meanwhile, the dust cloud continued to wheel around, revolving furiously. I could glimpse the silhouettes of the men; I could hear them swearing and coughing. Heraclitus was nowhere to be seen.

Then, in the driving rain, something drew near.

Two bright blue eyes. Lights in the darkness. A figure, all shadow and smoke, moved toward us.

"Heraclitus, is that you?" I said.

The shadow began to speak. The voice was faint and childish.

"I don't know who I am, I know what I am no longer. I am no longer a child, I am not your unfortunate sister, I am not an adolescent, I am none of the names that you give to your past. In just a few years, you have murdered the world's long childhood, it belonged to everyone and you have stolen it. There will be no more children. We will grow up too fast, just so we can defend ourselves from you. After a few years, we will learn to use your weapons and we will wage war against you. Our play soldiers will become real wars. Those who survive will grow old in an instant. Until one day, someone will decide that it makes no sense to go on. This is what you wanted, what you have created by pretending to be strong. You are all dead, impotent, defeated."

"Who are you?!" yelled Frido, and he fired his gun. The figure seemed to fly toward him, leaping upon him. I heard a terrified scream, then the click of a button.

An instant later, there was a huge explosion, a white-hot burst of heat and air that knocked me to the ground. When I managed to rise from the ground, in the core of the twisting dust cloud I saw flying bicycles, stones, strips of sheet metal, and other things that I prefer not to remember. The shed was gutted, and was burning furiously. The explosion had blown out all the windows in our house, and even the Cube had been damaged. It was riddled with cracks, the windows were raining shards of glass onto the lawn and onto me.

I don't remember everything.

Or I remember perfectly well how the house of games, my refuge, my all-too brief past exploded into the sky.

Perhaps it was Heraclitus who triggered the explosion with his switch; maybe someone else fired a gun, or else it was a regrettable accident, as the newspapers say.

Perhaps Lenora, or Angelo, or some ghost.

You can see us standing there, weeping, Mamma and me. Surrounded by a small army of policemen and firemen, while the dust of broken glass and the smoke from the flames prevent the dawn from arriving. It seemed as if it would always be night.

The pitiless eyes of the television cameras follow us, rummaging in the rubble, hunting hungrily for blood.

The cameras seek a scream to transform into chitchat and

rumors, newspaper headlines, the background music of complete indifference, Bach for the masses, violins for the injuries and harps for the children. Video tape number four.

A journalist moved toward the corpses covered with sheets, identical and white. An automaton of a policeman shooed him away. It was the handsome technician Gordon. In his gestures, in the excited words toward his comrades, there was clearly only one overriding concern.

To make sure that nobody learn how it happened, that none of them be dragged into it.

The same as it's been for so many years, the same as it's been with so many deaths.

Mamma was weeping like a little girl, and she leaned against me. I wanted to reassure her, tell her that this was all just a game, in the sun-dusted haze of the shed. Heraclitus was just pretending to be dead, and was snickering underneath his sheet. That Dad was hiding among the bicycles. That Giacinto was shooting a cork on a string out of a toy gun. That the police cars were just pressed-tin models, that the corpses were scarecrows, and that all this is just a movie, we can rewind it and watch it again whenever we want, on our giant-screen TV.

Or else, that I am looking out on the submerged city and that I am telling you this story, daughter of mine, the same age now as I was that night.

You can believe that those were just hard years, or else that they were the worst years in the history of the world. Years in which the world aged suddenly. And that, in aging, the world acquired only the selfishness and desperation of old age, not the wisdom and generosity.

In Closing

*I need to finish the book, said the girl in the forest.
I will write in tiny letters, and from up above the airplane
won't be able to read them.*

But her hand was trembling and the smoke blinded her.

*She composed sixteen bad pieces of poetry, then inspiration
arrived like a lancing glare, in the middle of the night, and she
wrote rapidly and furiously, as if there were little time left to
her.*

*The blond knight, Sir von Opfanwelingen, entered the red
forest and found a girl there, weeping as she stood by the ruins
of the house.*

*One day, someone will pay for all this, said the girl with the
dust-colored hair.*

*Little mermaid, said the emperor with a laugh, don't say
that, the world would never hurt little children.*

The knight's lance ripped through his throat.

*The knight, Sir von Opferdelingen, came to the shore of the
lake, and the lake was darker than he had ever seen it.*

*Behind the door that divided the water from the sky, he
heard a song.*

*The knight took off his armor and laid down his weapons,
and everyone saw how young he was, how tired.*

Drink, said a drop of water on a leaf.

On the day that commemorated the long-ago death of the

king, my father, I walked toward the broad still river, I set my guitar down upon the grass, and I walked into the water.

Let me embrace you, said the river.

When the water was already lapping around his chest, the knight saw that the girl from the forest had kindled a fire in the distance: a bonfire, or perhaps just a small candle.

She was waiting for someone.

Desire, a venerable teacher had once told him, is this: To wait beneath the stars for someone to return, alive, from the field of battle.

And the riverbank was crowded with flowers, and the water mirrored the stars, more than he had ever seen in his life.

Of course, no one got any sleep that night. I heard Mamma walking back and forth, and over the rhythm of her footsteps I heard the slow-paced melody of weeping. I listened to the voices of the policemen surrounding the house, the buzz of the electric eye beams, the noise of the steamshovel.

"I think we got to one of them in time," a voice was saying.

I walked out of the house. The rain had stopped, but the air was still filled with dust. A policeman began following, at a polite distance.

The meadow looked the same.

It was a cold, strange springtime, but it was the only one we had.

The spotlights looked like giant daisies, and they knifed through the darkness. In the reflection of those unexpected lights, the meadow creatures danced slowly: nocturnal moths, swarms of gnats, and oblique bats. The crickets were chirping away, flattered by that blinding stage, and a cloud of life was rising from the damp grass.

Their brief life, infancy and death in a single day.

They wouldn't waste an instant.

I walked on the grass, a light breeze in my face.

And yet it was so pretty here, where it's neither city nor country.

Dawn came. Suddenly, looking toward the little grove of trees, I saw her. This time she wasn't made of dust and smoke; she was real, a girl just like me, hesitant and pale. As I drew closer I noticed her mud-encrusted hair and her bloody hands. With a slight motion, she invited me to follow her.

We walked across the meadow, toward her home.

The grass was so tall and wet that it felt as if we were walking in water. She was flying, leaving a misty wake of vapor behind her.

When we got there, everything had changed.

The river was swollen with rain, and it was dammed by a barricade of fallen trees, mud, and garbage. It could no longer withstand the daily insults of humanity. And so it had overflowed its banks and invaded the forest, making a little lake in the pit of rubble. A still pool of dark water, riven by brief eddies. At the deepest part, by the light of dawn, I saw the tree of the cross. The cross was covered with water, but the branches of the elm tree rose high into the air, like the sails and rigging of a sunken ship.

And I saw the footsteps that led toward the water.

I followed them, until I was forced to kneel down on the muddy bank to peer in.

Oh my love, why did you listen to the siren's song? Wasn't my bad poetry enough for you? Didn't my love make you laugh hard enough?

I imagined you as you descended the staircase of mud, into the silence of the opening water.

The helmet and the sword remained on the riverbank, along with your dreams and your shattered beauty.

The crickets made their nest in the guitar, and his bandanna had become a red poppy.

My little sister appeared behind me, a reflection in the water. She showed me where to look.

There was a light, at the edge of the woods.

It was a red candle, in the shelter of a rock. The flame flickered in the light airs, and in the luminous halo of light there teemed a dust cloud of moths and gnats, winged phantoms and dragonflies, fairies and bacteria, fertile seeds and dead cells, and kernels of fallen stars, mists of lime-coated bones, and the tattered rags of the gods.

He had lighted the candle. It was an offering, a prayer to the meadow and to its irrepressible life.

To the crazy sacred grove to which we all belong.

Little Sister, I asked, tell me that candle was lighted recently.

Tell me that he is still near, that I will find him again, that I will hear his voice singing behind a door.

That's right, said the Dust Girl with a laugh. She flew close to me and gestured for me to look at my reflection in the water.

I saw that I had a wound on my temple.

A piece of shrapnel from the explosion, perhaps, and a drop of blood ran down my arm. I thought:

Good night, blood of mine.

I saw that my hair was full of dust, that my hands were covered with mud. My sister and I looked at one another, one beside the other, reflected in the water, and we were identical.

She tossed her hair away from her face and, pointing to my reflection, laughed.

She was beautiful.

She waved goodbye.
The water turned dark again, and the forest was empty.
And I understood that I would never see her again.

Stefano Benni is widely considered one of Italy's foremost novelists. His trademark mix of biting social satire and magical realism has turned each of his books into a national bestseller. His many novels include: *Bar Sport*, *The Company of the Celestini*, *The Cafe Beneath the Sea* and now the remarkably successful *Margherita Dolce Vita*. Benni is also the author of several volumes of essays and poetry and many collections of short stories. He lives in Bologna, Italy.

About Europa Editions

"To insist that if work is good, no matter what, people will read it? Crazy! But perhaps that's why I like Europa . . . They believe in what they are doing above everything. Viva Europa Editions!"
—ALICE SEBOLD, author of *The Lovely Bones*

"A new and, on first evidence, excellent source for European fiction for English-speaking readers."—JANET MASLIN, *The New York Times*

"Europa Editions has its first indie bestseller, Elena Ferrante's *The Days of Abandonment*."—*Publishers Weekly*

"We certainly like what we've seen so far."—*The Complete Review*

"A distinctly different brand of literary pleasure, thoughtfulness and, yes, even entertainment."—*The Ruminator*

"You could consider Europa Editions, the sprightly new publishing venture [...] based in New York, as a kind of book club for Americans who thirst after exciting foreign fiction."—*LA Weekly*

"Europa Editions invites English-speaking readers to 'experience all the color, the exuberance, the violence, the sounds and smells of the Mediterranean,' with an intriguing selection of the crème de la crème of continental noir."—*Murder by the Bye*

"Readers with a taste—even a need—for an occasional inky cup of bitter honesty should lap up *The Goodbye Kiss* . . . the first book of Carlotto's to be published in the United States by the increasingly impressive new Europa Editions."—*Chicago Tribune*

www.europaeditions.com

AVAILABLE NOW FROM EUROPA EDITIONS

The Jasmine Isle
Ioanna Karystiani
Fiction - 176 pp - $14.95 - isbn 1-933372-10-9

A modern love story with the force of an ancient Greek tragedy. Set on the spectacular Cycladic island of Andros, *The Jasmine Isle*, one of the finest literary achievements in contemporary Greek literature, recounts the story of the old sea wolf, Spyros Maltambès, and the beautiful Orsa Saltaferos, sentenced to marry a man she doesn't love and to watch while the man she does love is wed to another.

I Loved You for Your Voice
Sélim Nassib
Fiction - 256 pp - $14.95 - isbn 1-933372-07-9

"Om Kalthoum is great. She really is."—BOB DYLAN

Love, desire, and song set against the colorful backdrop of modern Egypt. The story of Egypt's greatest and most popular singer, Om Kalthoum, told through the eyes of the poet Ahmad Rami, who wrote her lyrics and loved her in vain all his life. This passionate tale of love and longing provides a key to understanding the soul, the aspirations and the disappointments of the Arab world.

The Days of Abandonment
Elena Ferrante
Fiction - 192 pp - $14.95 - isbn 1-933372-00-1

"Stunning . . . The raging, torrential voice of the author is something rare."
—JANET MASLIN, *The New York Times*

"I could not put this novel down. Elena Ferrante will blow you away."
—ALICE SEBOLD, author of *The Lovely Bones*

The gripping story of a woman's descent into devastating emptiness after being abandoned by her husband with two young children to care for.

Troubling Love
Elena Ferrante
Fiction - 144 pp - $14.95 - isbn 1-933372-16-8

"In tactile, beautifully restrained prose, Ferrante makes the domestic violence that tore [the protagonist's] household apart evident."—*Publishers Weekly*

"Ferrante has written the 'Great Neapolitan Novel.'"—*Il Corriere della Sera*

Delia's voyage of discovery through the chaotic streets and claustrophobic sitting rooms of contemporary Naples in search of the truth about her mother's untimely death.

www.europaeditions.com

Cooking with Fernet Branca
James Hamilton-Paterson
Fiction - 288 pp - $14.95 - isbn 1-933372-01-X

"A work of comic genius."—*The Independent*

Gerald Samper, an effete English snob, has his own private hilltop
in Tuscany where he wiles away his time working as a ghostwriter
for celebrities and inventing wholly original culinary concoctions.
Gerald's idyll is shattered by the arrival of Marta, on the run from a
crime-riddled former Soviet republic. A series of hilarious
misunderstandings brings this odd couple into ever closer and
more disastrous proximity.

Old Filth
Jane Gardam
Fiction - 256 pp - $14.95 - isbn 1-933372-13-3

"Jane Gardam's beautiful, vivid and defiantly funny novel is a
must."—*The Times*

Sir Edward Feathers has progressed from struggling young barrister
to wealthy expatriate lawyer to distinguished retired judge, living
out his last days in comfortable seclusion in Dorset. The engrossing
and moving account of his life, from birth in colonial Malaya, to
Wales, where he is sent as a "Raj orphan," to Oxford, his career
and marriage, parallels much of the 20th century's dramatic history.

Total Chaos
Jean-Claude Izzo
Fiction/Noir - 256 pp - $14.95 - isbn 1-933372-04-4

"Caught between pride and crime, racism and fraternity, tragedy and light, messy urbanization and generous beauty, the city for Montale is a Utopia, an ultimate port of call for exiles. There, he is torn between fatalism and revolt, despair and sensualism."
—*The Economist*

This first installment in the legendary *Marseilles Trilogy* sees Fabio Montale turning his back on a police force marred by corruption and racism and taking the fight against the Mafia into his own hands.

Chourmo
Jean-Claude Izzo
Fiction/Noir - 256 pp - $14.95 - isbn 1-933372-17-6

"Like the best noir writers—and he is among the best—Izzo not only has a keen eye for detail but also digs deep into what makes men weep."—*Time Out, New York*

Montale is dragged back into the mean streets of a violent, crime-infested Marseilles after the disappearance of his long lost cousin's young son.

The Goodbye Kiss
Massimo Carlotto
Fiction/Noir - 192 pp - $14.95 - isbn 1-933372-05-2

"The best living Italian crime writer."—*Il Manifesto*

An unscrupulous womanizer, as devoid of morals now as he once was full of idealistic fervor, returns to Italy where he is wanted for a series of crimes. To avoid prison he sells out his old friends, turns his back on his former ideals, and cuts deals with crooked cops. To earn himself the guise of respectability he is willing to go even further, maybe even as far as murder.

Death's Dark Abyss
Massimo Carlotto
Fiction/Noir - 192 pp - $14.95 - isbn 1-933372-18-4

"A narrative voice that in Lawrence Venuti's translation is cold and heartless—but, in a creepy way, fascinating."—*The New York Times*

A riveting drama of guilt, revenge, and justice, Massimo Carlotto's *Death's Dark Abyss* tells the story of two men and the savage crime that binds them. During a robbery, Raffaello Beggiato takes a young woman and her child hostage and later murders them. Beggiato is arrested, tried, and sentenced to life. The victims' father and husband, Silvano, plunges into a deepening abyss until the day the murderer seeks his pardon and Silvano begins to plot his revenge.

Hangover Square
Patrick Hamilton
Fiction/Noir - 280 pp - $14.95 - isbn 1-933372-06-0

"Hamilton is a sort of urban Thomas Hardy: always a pleasure to read, and as social historian he is unparalleled."—NICK HORNBY

Adrift in the grimy pubs of London at the outbreak of World War II, George Harvey Bone is hopelessly infatuated with Netta, a cold, contemptuous small-time actress. George also suffers from occasional blackouts. During these moments one thing is horribly clear: he must murder Netta.

Boot Tracks
Matthew F. Jones
Fiction/Noir - 208 pp - $14.95 - isbn 1-933372-11-7

"Mr. Jones has created a powerful blend of love and violence, of the grotesque and the tender."
—*The New York Times*

A commanding, stylishly written novel that tells the harrowing story of an assassination gone terribly wrong and the man and woman who are taking their last chance to find a safe place in a hostile world.

Love Burns
Edna Mazya
Fiction/Noir - 192 pp - $14.95 - isbn 1-933372-08-7

"Starts out as a psychological drama and becomes a strange, funny, unexpected hybrid: a farce thriller. A great book."—*Ma'ariv*

Ilan, a middle-aged professor of astrophysics, discovers that his young wife is having an affair. Terrified of losing her, he decides to confront her lover instead. Their meeting ends in the latter's murder—the unlikely murder weapon being Ilan's pipe—and in desperation, Ilan disposes of the body in the fresh grave of his kindergarten teacher. But when the body is discovered, the mayhem begins.

Departure Lounge
Chad Taylor
Fiction/Noir - 176 pp - $14.95 - isbn 1-933372-09-5

"Entropy noir . . . The hypnotic pull lies in the zigzag dance of its forlorn characters, casting a murky, uneasy sense of doom."
—*The Guardian*

A young woman mysteriously disappears. The lives of those she has left behind—family, acquaintances, and strangers intrigued by her disappearance—intersect to form a captivating latticework of coincidences and surprising twists of fate. Urban noir at its stylish and intelligent best.

Minotaur
Benjamin Tammuz
Fiction/Noir - 192 pp - $14.95 - isbn 1-933372-02-8

"A novel about the expectations and compromises that humans create for themselves . . . Very much in the manner of William Faulkner and Lawrence Durrell."—*The New York Times*

An Israeli secret agent falls hopelessly in love with a young English girl. Using his network of contacts and his professional expertise, he takes control of her life without ever revealing his identity. *Minotaur* is a complex and utterly original story about a solitary man driven from one side of Europe to the other by his obsession.

Dog Day
Alicia Giménez-Bartlett
Fiction/Noir - 208 pp - $14.95 - isbn 1-933372-14-1

"Giménez-Bartlett has discovered a world full of dark corners and hidden elements."—*ABC*

In this hardboiled fiction for dog lovers and lovers of dog mysteries, detective Petra Delicado and her maladroit sidekick, Garzon, investigate the murder of a tramp whose only friend is a mongrel dog named Freaky. One murder leads to another and Delicado finds herself involved in the sordid, dangerous world of fight dogs. *Dog Day* is first-rate entertainment.

The Big Question
Wolf Erlbruch
Children's Illustrated Fiction - 52 pp - $14.95 - isbn 1-933372-03-6

Named Best Book at the 2004 Children's Book Fair in
Bologna.

A stunningly beautiful and poetic illustrated book for children
that poses the biggest of all big questions: why am I here?
A chorus of voices—including the cat's, the baker's, the pilot's
and the soldier's—offers us some answers. But nothing is certain,
except that as we grow each one of us will pose the question
differently and be privy to different answers.

The Butterfly Workshop
Wolf Erlbruch
Children's Illustrated Fiction - 40 pp - $14.95 - isbn 1-933372-12-5

For children and adults alike: Odair, one of the "Designers of All
Things" and grandson of the esteemed inventor of the rainbow,
has been banished to the insect laboratory as punishment for his
overactive imagination. But he still dreams of one day creating a
cross between a bird and a flower. Then, after a helpful chat with
a dog . . .

Carte Blanche
Carlo Lucarelli
Fiction/Noir - 120 pp - $14.95 - isbn 1-933372-15-X

"Carlo Lucarelli is the great promise of Italian crime writing."
—*La Stampa*

April 1945, Italy. Commissario De Luca is heading up a dangerous investigation into the private lives of the rich and powerful during the frantic final days of the fascist republic. The hierarchy has guaranteed De Luca their full cooperation, so long as he arrests the "right" suspect. The house of cards built by Mussolini in the last months of World War II is collapsing and De Luca faces a world mired in sadistic sex, dirty money, drugs and murder.